The fifth book in the Keeping Days series

# A Nice Girl Like You

*a novel by*
## NORMA JOHNSTON

TEMPO BOOKS, NEW YORK

*For* JEAN KARL
*who thought of it first*

This Tempo Book contains the complete
text of the original hardcover edition.
It has been completely reset in a typeface
designed for easy reading, and was printed
from new film.

A NICE GIRL LIKE YOU

A Tempo Book / published by arrangement with
Atheneum Publishers

PRINTING HISTORY
Atheneum edition / 1980
Tempo edition / May 1982
Second printing / January 1983

ISBN: 0-441-57434-3

Tempo Books are published by Charter Communications, Inc.,
200 Madison Avenue, New York, N.Y. 10016.
Tempo Books are registered in the United States Patent Office.

PRINTED IN THE UNITED STATES OF AMERICA

# January

# I

ON MONDAY, JANUARY 11, 1917, WHEN I FINALLY WENT
back to school a week late from vacation, due to what
Gram called "tarnation too much socializing" and
Mother called the flu, I ran smack into the excitement
about Katie's sixteenth birthday party and the latest set
of ugly rumors about Paul Hodge.

Actually, on that Monday, I had plenty of other
things to occupy my mind. One of the drawbacks of
growing up in a neighborhood like West Farms, the
Bronx, where you have uncles and aunts and cousins
on every corner, is that you have a built-in family reputation to live up to—or live down, as the case may be. I
was Sarah Anne Albright, Bronwyn Sterling Albright's
daughter, and niece of that famous author, Letitia
Chambers Sterling; niece also of Sourpuss Sadie Albright, who'd been the bane of all local Latin students
before she had her stroke. I wasn't as strong-willed and

assertive (family translation: pigheaded) as Katie, who'd inherited the bossiness of that legendary Aunt Kate for whom she'd been named. I was "that nice little Albright girl," which explained why at ten minutes after three I was standing with forced politeness while Mr. Dirksen told me in precise detail what he thought of my shortcomings on my last Latin test.

"I'm sure your aunt, Miss Albright, would be glad to help you if you asked her," he finished acidly.

I did not need this, on top of having discovered in English class that Miss Olsen was spending this marking period on *The Merchant of Venice* and extensive forays into composition. "I know *you'll* do well," she said gaily, handing me a list of the assignments I'd already missed. I bit back the temptation to remind her that Aunt Tish was the writer in the family and not I.

Katie was waiting to walk home with me, and Katie kept waiting could have a caustic tongue. So I hurried down the hall, once Mr. Dirksen finished his lecture. Katie is not only my dearest friend, she is also, incongruously, my aunt, and being ten months my senior is very much in the habit of acting like Big Sister. I can understand why. Katie suffers from being kid sister to six siblings who range from my mother through Uncle Ben the lawyer, Aunt Tish the writer, and Aunt Marnie the ex-tomboy, now the mother of four boys. Not to mention Peter the zoologist and Melissa, who, as Gram says, "majored in boys and foolishness" in school. All exuberant and opinionated; all (except Tish who lives in England) living within a few blocks of each other. They helped Gram and Gramp bring Katie up—and Katie, having nobody younger in her own house to boss, instinctively does to me as she's been done to. I can understand it, but that doesn't always make it easier to put up with.

The girls' cloakroom was empty, which meant Katie must be already at the door. Nonetheless, I stole a moment for a swift survey in the mirror. I had hoped my week's incarceration might have left me looking interestingly pale and fragile, but the mirror told me clearly that I was still plain Saranne Albright, with the dark hair that refused to wave, and the sprinkling of freckles on the sallow skin. When reporters describe Aunt Tish, who inherited this same complexion, they refer to it as olive-gold and make it sound romantic. It's wonderful how fame can turn a liability into an asset.

"Kid, aren't you ever coming?" Katie's face loomed behind mine in the mirror. "Come on, the meeting must have already started!"

"What meeting?"

"Browning Society. Weren't you listening at the lunch table?"

"I thought all we talked about at lunch was your birthday party. And I thought I missed a Browning meeting just last week."

"You did. This is special to make plans for Friday night."

I looked at Katie blankly, and she shook her head

and thrust a handbill at me. I stared at it, and for a moment the room spun.

!!! BROWNING SOCIETY OPEN MEETING
FRIDAY NIGHT !!!
*Public Invited!*
*Debate—Refreshments—Social Hour!*
The Changing Role of Women, in Literature and Life
—Natural or Unnatural?

DEBATE between MARK SCHERMERHORN
SCHUYLER III of Browning Society
and noted alumna
BRONWYN STERLING ALBRIGHT!!!

MSS III, Congressman Schuyler's son, new to our school this fall and promptly elected president of Browning Society in this, his senior year, happens to have an old-fashioned sense of masculine superiority . . . and to be the only reason I wanted to be in Browning Society at all. And Bronwyn Albright, past Browning President, noted suffragette and public speaker, wife of the prominent attorney, happens to be my mother.

"I gather you didn't know," Katie said drily, and then, with concern, "Saranne, are you all right?"

"I'm fine," I said, with as much dignity as I could manage.

"I'm surprised Bron didn't tell you."

"She probably forgot. I was sick all last week, remember? And on Sunday, when we ate at your house, all anybody talked about was your party, and Melissa's flirting, and the War, and how we haven't heard from Aunt Tish for months. Besides, Mother doesn't realize it embarrasses me sometimes to have her so—notorious. And don't you dare go telling her, Katie Sterling!"

". . . SENT INVITATIONS TO THE NEWSPAPERS," MARK Schuyler was saying as we slid into seats in the rear. "It should be worth a story. Noted old grad returns to scene of former triumphs and all that."

"Magnanimous of him, wasn't it?" Tim Molloy, in the seat beside me, whispered drily. He was an old friend, the brother of Stella Molloy, who married my own half-brother Junius. I looked at Tim blankly, and he grinned with mischief. "Don't you know MSS III's itching to be known as the man who bested Bronwyn Albright in debate?"

My heart sank. I tried to blot out the debate by focusing on Mark Schuyler's dark-gold hair and deep hazel eyes, with those incredible lashes that are totally unfair for a man to have. But it didn't work.

There were always refreshments at Browning Society evening programs, but this time Mark was speaking of ordering cakes and tea sandwiches from a caterer. "My father has offered to underwrite expenses," he said casually.

As a concerted cheer of approval went up, I turned to look at Katie, who was whispering something.

"Now do you see why my party's got to be a humdinger? Times are changing. And we're growing up."

". . . ought to have ushers Friday," Mark was saying. "To hand out programs, make guests from the community feel at home. Are there any volunteers?"

Katie's hand shot up at once. So, to everyone's astonishment—including my own—did mine.

"Saranne Albright, of course." Miss Olsen, calling off names to be recorded, smiled at me. "We're all looking forward to Friday. You must be very proud of your mother, dear."

I ALMOST DROPPED MY BOOKS WHEN MARK FELL INTO STEP beside me after the meeting ended. "I didn't realize my noted opponent is your mother. Should be an interesting evening for you! Who will you root for?"

I reached for the enigmatic smile Melissa used to tantalize her beaux. "That would be telling."

"You're a member of the present Browning Society. It's your duty to root for me, Albright."

"Her name's Saranne," Katie said acidly. "Or don't you believe in treating us females like ladies?"

Mark gave her a challenging glance. "I thought 'you females' wanted to be treated like men. Or aren't you interested in rights for women, *Miss* Sterling?"

Katie was caught between crusades, and she didn't like it. Her black eyes snapped.

"OK, OK, save the War Between the Sexes for Friday, will you?" Tim came up between them, grinning. "Personally, I've had enough of Moral Uplift. How about stopping by the Majestic for the late matinee on the way home. Dutch," he added, as if we didn't know. "Mary Hayes's new picture's just opened."

It was not the first time we'd done this, but it was the first time Mark had joined us. Yet he fell in beside us as a matter of course. "What's so special about a Mary Hayes picture?" he asked.

"She's Paul Hodge's sister," Katie said, as if that said it all. Which in a way it did. Mark looked puzzled.

"You mean the Hodge who got suspended three days last week because Dirksen thought he was going to take a swing at him?"

"The same. Though I don't think even Hodge would waste effort taking a poke at that old maid in breeches. He was sore because Dirksen kept insisting it would not be in U.S. interest to get involved in the European War, and Hodge is rabid about how we ought to help the French and English." Tim was an expert on the Hodges, living next door to them. "Mary Hodge was quite a fly in the ointment back in her Browning days, according to my sister Stella. Anyway, one night there was a helluva row." Tim grinned reminiscently. "I was only five years old, but I still remember. It shook the walls! The next day Mary was gone, and next thing you know she turned up on the flickering screen as Mary Hayes, being promoted as 'The Girl with the Curl' to rival Mary Pickford. You could have knocked the neighborhood over with a feather. And she hasn't darkened the doors of West Farms since."

The Majestic Theater on Tremont Street had its

billboards papered with pictures of Mary Hayes's mischievous smile and red-gold curls. Katie and I reached for our purses, but Mark was quicker. "Permit me," he said smoothly, and bought four tickets. Katie raised her eyebrows at me, and Tim looked faintly wary.

Katie poked me. "You're daydreaming again. Come on, the picture's starting."

I turned from watching a slender boy with ragged gold hair, who had brushed past us toward the exit, his face averted. "I think that was Paul Hodge. It must be funny, seeing your sister on a movie screen."

"About the same as seeing Bron on a lecture platform, or reading Tish's books," Katie said indifferently. "Anyway, I'm glad he's gone. I'd hate to have to sit next to him. He scares me."

I felt scared, in a different way, finding myself sitting between Tim and Mark; I was very conscious of Mark's nearness. On his other side, Katie was nonchalant. But soon I forgot everything except the pictures flickering on the screen.

Mary Hayes's new picture was a War one, laid in occupied France. Uncle Anthony, Aunt Tish's English husband, was fighting somewhere there. In her last letter, Aunt Tish had said that he was training to be a pilot. That had been six months ago, and since then—nothing.

The piano player's music rose to a crescendo. On the screen a plane crashed into a French farmhouse where we knew Mary Hayes was nursing a wounded flier. Flames belched out, consuming the thatched roof, blackening the sky. I closed my eyes.

Was it so terribly wrong to wish I could just . . . see the nice things in life . . . and not get so torn by all the things that could go so very wrong?

"You can open your eyes now," Tim's voice said drily. "The picture's over."

We emerged into January sleet.

"Stop by my house," Tim said. "We're closest. Ma'll dry you off." Mark excused himself, but Katie and I accepted. The Molloy house was dark, but we went in anyway, just to catch our breath before we went on. I was still thinking about the movie.

"Come on, Saranne," he said good-naturedly, "come back from the flames of France." And then, in an altered tone, "Good gosh, those *are* flames!"

We stared with him, stunned, through the window to the orange glow coming from the windows of the Hodge house next door.

Only a moment, and then we were pelting out the door. Or at least Tim and I were; behind us I heard Katie, the practical, cranking the phone to call the fire department. We pounded across the icy lawn, up slippery steps, burst through the Hodge back door.

The kitchen was filled with smoke. But through it I could make out Mr. Hodge slumped in an armchair, Paul, standing over him, frozen at our approach.

Tim shoved him aside roughly. "Get out! I'll get your father!" Already he was sliding an arm beneath Mr. Hodge's heavy one. I took hold of Paul and steered him toward the door. He moved like a sleepwalker, dazed with shock. Mr. Hodge was overcome from other causes—I could smell the alcohol fumes, even through the smoke. We emerged, choking, as sirens shrieked and the neighborhood's new motorized fire truck screeched to a halt.

Katie came running over, her arms full of blankets. "Get these on him." She jerked her head towards Paul. Sleet was pelting down harder now.

Firemen loomed beside us, and suddenly everything was out of our hands. They were leading Paul off, trying to shake him alert, questioning him. They had gotten Mr. Hodge's inert bulk onto a stretcher. An ambulance screamed. Tim's parents were there, clucking over us, marching us off to be treated like children and bundled into dry clothes and fed hot food. Dad arrived to escort me home, and Uncle Ben for Katie; he lived next door to her, in the little house that had once been Aunt Kate's.

In the bustle, Katie paused beside me and spoke in a lowered voice. "Saranne . . . how do you suppose that fire got started? Tim said Paul was just standing there—is that true?"

"He was stunned, I think—" I broke off. "Katie Sterling, you're not suggesting—?"

"I'm not suggesting anything," Katie said in an odd voice. "But he did set fires when he was little. I saw him do it, once, in the vacant lot. But I was scared, and I never told anyone. Not even you."

The picture her words conjured whirled in my

brain that night, along with the pictures of Mary Hayes in a flaming farmhouse in France.

Along about midnight, the sleet turned to snow. We were probably in for a blizzard; they were always likely around Katie's birthday. Katie'd been born in one. We'd grown up hearing stories of how Aunt Kate had climbed through an upper window of her house and slid off the roof on her best tea tray to help Aunt Tish, then barely the age I was now, deliver Katie when the doctor couldn't get through the storm in time. . . . Why was I thinking of Aunt Tish so much today? I scarcely knew her. She'd gone to England with a former teacher who was on a writing and lecture tour, had published her own first book there, and had married. She'd come back twice, most recently bringing an enchanting two-year-old daughter. I had vague memories of a slim blonde girl-woman with dark eyes that were almost dazzlingly alive; of a tall, bronzed, gallant-looking man. That had been six years ago. She had planned to come again, the autumn of 1914. Only that August the Kaiser's troops had marched through Belgium on their way to France, and Britain as Belgium's ally had been catapulted into war.

"HEAR YOU HAD SOME EXCITEMENT YESTERDAY," MARK said, stopping beside Tim and me on our way to lunch the next day. "I guess I should have come home with you after all. Is it true Hodge set the fire himself?"

We just stared at him. My mouth felt dry. "Where did you hear that?"

Mark shrugged. "I thought it was common knowledge. My dad was talking to some fellows down at the precinct house; they said there's an investigation going on pending charges."

"IT'S TRUE," DAD SAID AT DINNER. BEING AN ATTORNEY, HE was often at the courthouse and heard police gossip. "Seems the boy keeps insisting it was an accident, but gives no explanation. And he *was* standing there."

Mother gave a faint soft sound. "But that's terrible . . . Sidney, Mr. Hodge was *sitting* there, passed out cold."

"I know," Dad said.

Junius and Stella were there, and my small niece and nephew. And Aunt Sadie, who'd lived with us since her stroke last fall. For a moment, there was something in the air, not just suspicion but something strange, some secret knowledge like a spiderweb that ran between the eyes of the adults but shut me out. Then Stella said, in that decided way of hers, "I don't believe it. Paul's wild, but that's all," and Aunt Sadie started her slurred-speech rendition of all Paul Hodge's sins, and Junius interrupted, "Has anyone heard from Tish yet?" which changed the subject from one difficult topic to another.

I didn't dream that night, but I didn't sleep much, either. I worked doggedly at the despised Latin and made a dent in *The Merchant of Venice*, but not the composition.

"A stupid story about a girl who's forced to marry

whoever can choose which locked casket contains her picture," Katie had said disparagingly of the play. She'd had to read it the year before. "If I was her, I'd have refused to do it. She wasn't such a fool in the end, though; she's the only one in the play who had real brains."

Reading, I could see what Katie meant. Portia was beautiful, witty, warm, and wise; she made me think, as a matter of fact, of my mother. But there was much more to the play than her strange courtship. For to woo her, the impecunious suitor, Bassanio, had to turn to his merchant friend Antonio for money . . . and Antonio, his fortune all at sea, in turn borrowed from the Jewish moneylender, Shylock. The bond, "a merry jest," a pound of Antonio's flesh if the debt was not paid in time. Bassanio won Portia both by way of caskets and by way of the heart, but their joy turned tragic because Antonio's ships were lost at sea. The bond was forfeit, and Shylock, venomous over past ill-treatment at the hands of Christians, was determined to exact his pound of flesh. It lay to Portia, disguised as a young lawyer, to find a way to save her bridegroom's friend.

"In what way does the society of Venice mirror the society in which we live?" Miss Olsen had asked me to write. I did not know.

IN THE MORNING, DAD LEARNED PAUL HODGE HAD NOT been charged because there was no evidence against him. "Thank God," Mother murmured, looking shaken. But he was not in school, and nine people out of ten there were taking "no evidence" to mean not "innocent" but "not provable."

Katie looked at me. "What's the matter, Saranne? You look queer."

I shook my head. "It doesn't make sense . . . why would he have been standing there? Why wouldn't he have gotten out? He could have been killed himself. . . . Can't we talk about something else?"

Katie looked skeptical, but accepted the change of subject. She switched to her party. "I tried for an all-nighter. Appropriate," she said wickedly, referring to the fact that she'd been born at midnight. "But Mama's not senile enough to fall for that one yet. But we are going to have dancing and a midnight supper." There were envious groans all around the lunch table, and I could see Abby Munroe and the Cartwright girls mentally planning how to enveigle new party frocks.

"However did you manage?"

"I guess Mama's resistance is worn down after seven kids. Actually, it was Melissa and Peter who made her admit I'm not an infant any more. We're carting the furniture up to the attic, the way we did for Marnie's wedding reception. You remember." That had been ten years ago, but everyone nodded. In this neighborhood, we all share common memories.

Abby Munroe's face looked awed. "I still remember peeking from the stairs, watching Mary Hayes dance the Hesitation with your brother Ben in her blue chiffon. That was right before she ran away, wasn't it? Gee, it seems weird, having a movie actress from our neighborhood."

Katie sniffed. "Hayes or Hodge, I personally don't think they add so much to the neighborhood's social tone."

Abby, having been snubbed, had to get her own back. "Aren't you going to ask Paul Hodge to your party?" she asked blandly.

"I certainly am not, so I hope you weren't pining for it, Abby Munroe!"

Abby shuddered. "Glory, no. He scares me. Those eyes! And now his setting a fire that could have killed his father—"

"But he didn't," I said involuntarily. "The police said so. They let him go."

There was a chorus of groans. "Saranne, don't be naive. That just means they couldn't prove anything, any more than they could prove he set those fires when he was small. There were no witnesses."

Katie was looking at me steadily. I remembered how she'd said she'd seen him start a fire and never told.

"Anyway," Katie said deliberately, "look at the things he *has* done. I tell you, I'm afraid of him, and I'm afraid of what worse things he may do someday."

"Besides," Abby added as though that clinched it, "he's a Hodge."

I knew what that meant. The Hodges were an old West Farms family and everyone's despair. Mr. Hodge had begun to drink steadily, right after Mary Hayes left home. The Hodge place never looked well-kept. Mrs. Hodge's clothes were always a bit too bright. I'd heard tales of the furor Paul's married sister had caused, turning up in a see-through blouse for classes at the secretarial school Gramp owned. Over all of it, the same rueful irritated shrug: *What could you expect? That's the Hodges.*

"You know what it makes me think of?" I heard my own voice saying. "That speech in *The Merchant of Venice* when Shylock tells how he's despised, just because he's a Jew. And how he might as well *do* evil, since it's expected, and he's already condemned for it. *That's* how our society here resembles Venice."

There was an openmouthed moment, and then Katie said sardonically, "Saranne, our Little Defender of the Underdog."

# February

# II

BEFORE KATIE'S PARTY CAME MOTHER'S DEBATE WITH MISS III. I wasn't looking forward to it. I half-hoped it would snow some more, so the whole thing would be postponed or, better still, called off. But there was not a cloud in the cold bright sky on Friday morning.

Dad grinned at Mother as she sat frowning over her notes at the breakfast table. "Don't tell me *you're* getting nervous!"

"I feel like a ghost," Mother muttered darkly, "returning to past scenes of triumph. Too much to live up to! Did you see the publicity in the *Times* this morning? I just hope I don't disgrace you all!"

"Nonsense!" Aunt Sadie said decidedly. "Wait till you get on that platform, girl. Sound of the gavel's like an alarm bell to a fire horse."

"I hope so. Just be sure you're there to give me moral support."

"Try'n stop me," Aunt Sadie said grimly. She was one of the old-time suffragettes, but hadn't gone out in public much since her stroke, so her emerging tonight was a tribute to my mother. Family legend recounted her outrage at my parents' marriage, because Dad had been a longtime widower with Sadie his housekeeper, but those days were now long gone. "Young whippersnapper," she said, referring to Mark Schermerhorn Schuyler III, and she made me read aloud the write-up in the paper.

"I don't know." Dad's eyes twinkled. "He's Congressman Schuyler's son, you know, and Sherm's a big gun in the political machine. I'll wager Sonny's expected to follow in his footsteps."

I WAS VERY CONSCIOUS OF THE TICKING OF CLOCKS ALL that day. They brought lunchtime, where everyone talked about the debate. Three o'clock; home from school with a Katie, who seemed not herself, alternately a chatterbox and silent. Four o'clock, tea at the kitchen table and having to be polite when Aunt Sadie plunked herself down to brief mother on arguments for the debate. Hating myself for being resentful of Aunt Sadie's disparaging contempt toward the "young whippersnapper"; for wishing Aunt Sadie wasn't going with us tonight; for not wanting to be identified before . . . people . . . as Sourpuss Sadie's niece, Bronwyn Albright's daughter.

Five o'clock, cooking dinner so Mother could work her nervous energies off in private. Five-thirty, dishing up, seeing Mother emerge from her bedroom radiant in coral silk. Seeing Dad gaze at her with pride. Wondering if . . . somebody . . . would ever, *could* ever look at me like that.

Seven o'clock, walking to the high school, being introduced to Mark's parents by my father, who knows everyone. Mark's father, like a matinee idol, all tanned skin and gleaming teeth. Mark in a suit I hadn't seen before, which made him look like a college junior. Katie, with her hair pinned up by one of Melissa's Spanish combs, whispering, "I got out of the house before Mama saw me. She won't make a scene in public, so she's livid, but at least I'm safe!"

Gram like a brisk bird, eyes bright, torn between indignation at Katie and pride in my mother. Gramps and Dad, who were best friends long before being in-laws, beaming with pride. Family all over the place—the Sterlings and the Albrights were out in force, all except Aunt Tish, who was across a war-tossed sea.

I wondered why I was suddenly thinking in phrases that could have come from one of Aunt Tish's novels. But I didn't have to wonder about my turbulence of feelings. I didn't want Mother to fail in her debate. But I didn't want Mark Schuyler to fail either!

The assembly hall was crowded. Here and there were brisk young men with notebooks, probably the reporters Mark had invited. Mark himself, all at once, was at my elbow. "Well, Miss Albright, aren't you going to introduce me to your mother?" There was a teasing intimacy to his voice, as if referring to an earlier private joke between us.

I did not perform the requested service with the poise I longed for. And I cringed as Mother used her queenly, public voice. "So this is the famous MSS III."

"Don't tell me Sarah Anne's been prejudicing you against your opponent in advance."

"You forget, I read the Browning Society Quarterly," Mother said drily. "Cover to cover. I've been wanting to discuss a few points with you."

"And I've been looking forward to the honor of tonight." He glanced at the timepiece his father had given him for Christmas. "It's time we were beginning. May I escort you?" He offered Mother his arm, and they swept off.

Miss Olsen, on the bunting-draped platform, rapped for order. The reporters settled themselves in the front row. "Ladies and gentlemen—that includes faculty, administration, parents, honored guests and, I hope, students!" There was a ripple of laughter. "I am delighted to welcome you on behalf of the Browning Society. As faculty advisor, I have this privilege because our president will be featured prominently, and partisanly, in the program." Her eyes twinkled. "I hope perhaps his asking me to be here indicates a softening in his stance against the equality of women!" Again laughter. I began to relax.

Miss Olsen gave a brief, charming introduction of my mother, repeating biographical data everybody knew. Mother rose, bowed, smiled. Miss Olsen did likewise for MSS III. He repeated Mother's performance.

Katie poked me. "When she mentioned Congressman Schuyler, I thought for a minute he was going to stand and take a bow!" Gram hissed for silence.

On the platform, a polite skirmish was ensuing over who was to speak first. Mark was making the grand gesture, and Mother shook her head. "By all means, do let Mr. Schuyler speak first. Men are by now so habituated to leading the way." Her wry tone brought a delightful chuckle from the audience. I saw a flicker of annoyance in Mark's eyes.

He responded with the instant recovery of an experienced debater. "May I point out what I am sure my distinguished opponent already knows—that the custom of male precedence from time immemorial has sprung from the man, being biologically stronger, preceding the woman for her safety and protection. When the opposite order would best ensure that, the rule in all civilized societies has been, 'Women and children first.'"

He settled himself at the lectern as easily as at a regular Browning meeting. "And at the risk of seeming rude, I must respectfully beg to differ with a reference our faculty advisor just made. I am not against equality for women. On the contrary, I believe that in many spheres the ladies are not our equals but our superiors. It is against the loss, the coarsening, of those special qualities that I wish to speak." He smiled charmingly. "Contrary to rumor, you know, the real subject here is not voting, or equality, but men's and women's roles and purposes in life. And literature." He swept a mock-teasing bow in the direction of Miss Olsen and my mother, and I saw a familiar steely glint creep into her eyes.

That set the tone for his speech—ironic, gracious, a comedy of manners. With heavy emphasis on the natural delicacy, purity, fineness of women, which would be lost if they were forced into contact with the harsh realities of public life. Very complimentary. Everyone settled down and felt comfortable, enjoyed themselves.

Except Aunt Sadie. And Mother. And me. I couldn't put my finger on why. Because everything Mark was saying was respectful, was admiring, was pedestal-raising. Was—oh, I'll be honest, exactly the kind of things I wanted to hear him say, personally, about me.

And all at once I realized what was bothering me. The implication was that those qualities in women should be preserved because *men* needed them there— not because they were worth preserving intrinsically, or for the women's sake. Furthermore, those women he was talking about might be Mark's mother and grandmother and cousins. They certainly weren't mine.

Mother had worked when she was young. She was a suffragette, much in demand as a speaker now, yet our home hadn't lost any—what was it Mark called it?— beneficent nurturing influence. Gram, sitting with her lips tight, had been running the Sterling Secretarial School side by side with Gramp for years. And what about Aunt Sadie, who'd been teacher and suffragette; what about Miss Olsen and Aunt Tish's writer-friend Marguerite Finchler Owens? What about Aunt Tish herself? None of them were less than womanly, less than ladies.

Mark, circling back to his opening remarks, was referring to the War. Cessation of difference in men's and women's roles, everyone's doing the same things, being treated the same—wouldn't that mean women being forced into the armed services, no longer being safely behind the lines, protected?

He had touched an old fear. There was a ripple, like cold air, through the auditorium.

Mother stood up. "Forgive me if I wish my esteemed opponent was as well versed in history as in old arguments," she said in a silvery voice that filled me with foreboding. "My ancestors, like his, crossed the ocean in small ships to settle here in the 1620s, and from what I've read, their lives weren't particularly sheltered. Nor were those of the pioneer women who crossed the plains, nor those who lived through the American Revolution or the Civil War."

The reporters in the front row straightened, scenting battle. A voice somewhere opined that war today was different.

"Yes, it is," Mother said quietly. "There is no 'behind the lines' anymore." She stopped, and her manner made a silence settle. "Forgive me for speaking personally, but I have a sister who is *in* the War, married to an Englishman who has been at the front since the autumn of 1914. She is not being sheltered by her sex or her position or the fact that she does not have the vote. Nor are the French and Belgian women mentioned in her husband's letters. And if, as may well happen, the War should come to where she is, she will pick up a gun, as those women did. Or fight side by side with her men-folk in the trenches. As I would. As, I am quite sure, would every woman here."

There was a different kind of stillness now as Mother went deeper into her subject. The reporters were scribbling furiously, all but one far to the side who had stopped writing entirely.

"My brother Peter," Mother said finally, "among various other livestock with which he has afflicted us, has a crow." A burst of laughter cut the stillness. "He began as a house pet, but as he grew Peter let him loose outside. If Iago had been kept confined, he would never have gotten the strength of his wings, or been able to take care of himself when need arose, or realized all the potential the good Lord put into crows. I submit that confining humans—any humans—to specific narrow roles is as much a sin against their natures as it would be for crows." She sat down to a tumult of applause.

Miss Olsen invited everyone to the library for re-freshments, and the program at last was over. Mother stepped off the platform to be engulfed in reporters and relations. My eyes strayed towards Mark. He was still on the platform, looking at his father, but Congressman Schuyler was shaking hands with voters.

"Poor mug," Katie said, meaning Mark, and pushed off toward him. Probably she was reminding him of host responsibilities at the refreshment table. Dad was trying to propel Mother in that direction, too. They were stopped by the reporter I'd seen put away his note-book. Mother stared, started, threw her arms around him with a cry of delight.

"Kenneth! Ken Latham! What are you doing in New York?"

"I've just moved back from Boston. Had a chance to buy into a publishing firm in the city. I always did think I'd like the book business better than newspaper editing." Mr. Latham was shaking hands all round. "I saw in the paper about the debate, and of course, as an old Browning hand, I had to come." His voice changed. "Bronwyn, what do you hear from your sister?"

He meant Aunt Tish, of course. There was a momentary silence.

"We'll probably be hearing something any day," Gram said, brightly.

"I'm starved," I announced loudly, trying to overcome what seemed to be an awkward moment.

I got laughed at, but the tension was dissolved. We went to the library, where a little court formed around Mother. The lace-covered refreshment table blazed with candles, offering Congressman Schuyler's elegant catered spread, and Mark was hurrying about looking preoccupied.

"I—want to offer the compliments of the loyal opposition," I said, striving for the light touch. "You upheld the honor of the school very well."

"Oh. Yes. Thank you." Mark was actually curt. For a moment after he turned away I stared after him, my face stinging, and then common sense returned. He hadn't been snubbing *me;* he'd hardly seen me. He was angry; he was upset. Because of *Mother?*

But every word she said was true, a little voice inside me said, and if he didn't like to hear it. . . . I didn't like what I myself was feeling.

I wandered back towards my parents, feeling forlorn. The circle around Mother had thinned, and she had turned back into her private self, relaxed and sipping punch. Dad strolled off to talk to Gramp and Mr. Latham. Mother scanned my face. "You look tired. I hope you haven't overdone, this week, after being sick."

"I'm all right."

"Ah, Mrs. Albright. And Sarah Anne, isn't it?" Congressman Schuyler was before us, holding out his hand. "You must be very proud of your mother, young lady. Mrs. Albright, as one public speaker to another, I wonder if I might have a few words with you about your debate?"

Mr. Schuyler was standing facing my mother, but he turned slightly to throw at me that cool patronizing smile I hated when I saw it on Mark's face. It was definitely a dismissal. I felt about two inches tall.

Mother's fingertips rested, ever so lightly, on my arm. Her head came up in a way I knew well, but her voice was sweet as honey. "Oh, I don't mind my daughter hearing any critiques of my debating. Do go on with what you were saying, Mr. Schuyler."

The congressman shrugged charmingly. "I was only going to ask if you didn't think you'd been a mite hard on the lad. I know you ladies are adept at tugging the heart with your emotional appeals, but wasn't it a bit unfair to use them against a boy? After all, for you, tonight was an amusing little excursion into the past, but he is the President of Browning Society now, and it was a bit shaming for him."

"What was?" Mother asked very softly. "Being defeated? By a woman? Because he's being groomed for a political career, as I am not, and he did not quite live up to your demands? Or is it because you don't believe he *can* live up to them without some help, and is that why you think I should have gracefully thrown the debate and let him win?"

Mr. Schuyler's smile didn't move a muscle, but his tan suddenly looked artificial. He didn't make a sound. Somebody gave a faint, sharp cry. It was me, because beyond Mr. Schuyler I could see what he did not.

Mark. Mark, coming toward us and freezing as he heard his father's words, his condescending tone, and Mother's level-voiced retort. For an instant that nonchalant, suave façade was gone, and I saw fleetingly, not the great MSS III, but a human being pressured into a predetermined pattern just as surely, and perhaps as destructively, as Paul Hodge. It was at that moment that I ceased to be intimidated by Mark Schuyler . . . and that I finally acknowledged to myself my feelings for him.

I DIDN'T KNOW WHAT I WAS GOING TO DO ABOUT THAT realization or those feelings. What I was not going to do was let Katie find them out. And I wasn't going to let myself feel overpowered at her birthday party, when there was every chance in the world Mark would be there. I didn't know who was on the invitation list, and didn't ask, for I was afraid her boundless curiosity would ferret out why. Katie's help in getting Mark to notice me could be invaluable, but it could also be embarrassing.

Fortunately, Katie was so wrapped up in her party plans she didn't notice I was hiding anything. The party was turning into a Hippodrome spectacular.


"MAMA'S RESISTANCE IS GETTING WEAK IN HER OLD AGE." Mother chuckled. "You should have heard how she carried on when we wanted evening parties before we were seventeen!"

"I guess after Melissa she's used to anything." It was a family joke that the only reason Melissa wasn't married at sixteen was that New York State did not permit polygamy.

Between Melissa and Katie, Gram's motor was sputtering steadily. She worked in the secretarial school office till midafternoon; but five minutes after she got home, she'd be on the phone to Mother, letting off her version of whatever conflict Katie'd been exploding about all day. By the weekend before the party, the air around their house was incandescent.

"Katie's making dance cards," I reported Friday at the dinner table. "Or rather, she maneuvered Abby and me into making them while she bossed the job." I groaned, rubbing my arm. "Do you know what it's like to do Old English lettering all afternoon?"

Aunt Sadie snorted. "I'm surprised Eva's letting a child of hers carry on like that so young. Let alone that red spangled dress she got her. Eva must be getting senile."

Mother's lips tightened. Aunt Sadie had never cared who heard her malicious digs, and Dad's presence was the only thing that ever held her back. But Dad was down at the Lawyers' Club tonight.

"After dinner," Mother said brightly, "let's walk up to Gram's and see how things are going." She knew Aunt Sadie wouldn't come.

MOTHER AND I WALKED INTO GRAM'S KITCHEN TO FIND A row in progress. "I won't have him!" Katie was shouting. "He'll spoil everything."

"Don't like him any better'n you do," Gram retorted. "All the same, have to have him. Part of the neighborhood. Mother been in Altar Guild with me for thirty-five years." She was clipping off her sentences in the way that showed her dander was aroused.

"What's the matter?" Mother asked. Katie tossed her head.

"Mama's trying to make me ask Paul Hodge to the party. I'm not going to have my birthday party turn into a brawl."

"And who are you to go passing judgement like that, young lady?" Gram's eyes snapped. "Boy's been caught smoking, talking back, got suspended for that'n cutting school. Don't see he's done anything worse'n your own brothers have."

"What do you call setting fire to his own house?" Katie countered darkly.

"Wasn't proved. You're passing judgement again."

Katie switched arguments. "You promised me this could be a special party. Paul Hodge will show up like a factory hand, all over grease!"

"Should think you could give him credit, having the gumption to go out and get a job." Gram drew herself up. "Suit yourself. But there'll be no party, grand or otherwise, less'n you stop singling neighbors out to be rejected."

Katie's jaw dropped.

"Didn't raise no child of mine to be a snob and cause hurt feelings," Gram said flatly. She stalked out, and Mother followed.

"What brought all that on?" I asked cautiously.

Katie jerked a chair out and sat down. "I made the mistake of leaving my invitation list out, and Mama read it. Honestly, you'd think I'd be entitled to some privacy. Not to mention my own judgement! Anyway, she saw that Paul's name had been left off. And she'd just come home from Altar Guild, where Mrs. Hodge had been burbling about my lovely party."

"I don't see why the big fuss," I said practically. "What if Paul does come looking like he just got off the boat? The kids are used to it."

Katie, unexpectedly, blushed.

"Katherine Allison Sterling, you are up to something."

"Don't be ridiculous."

"Ridiculous, my Aunt Sadie. Let me see that invitation list."

"I tore it up and burned it. And don't you dare tell me that was a dramatic gesture," Katie said darkly. "I've already heard enough on that score from Mama. Anyway, I don't know why Mama's tender feelings are aroused. Mrs. Hodge doesn't care two hoots about her rotten kid, and Mama knows it."

"Maybe she's thinking about the rotten kid."

"Waste of energy," Katie snorted. "He's got a hide like a rhinoceros."

"What's the matter with *your* skin? It doesn't usually rattle you so when Gram goes on a righteousness crusade. Or when there're waifs and strays around. In our family that's not unusual."

"That's just it. There's got to be a stop somewhere. Especially now that—oh, Saranne, you just don't understand." Katie sounded remarkably like me. She completed the transformation by bursting into tears. "Mama's being impossible. You've got to help me. She's trying to make me fill in the neck of my new dress, on account of your Aunt Sadie's nasty cracks. And she's not at all enthusiastic about dance programmes. The only thing that got her off that subject was finding the invitation list, and you know what happened then."

GRAM AND KATIE WERE STILL ON THE OUTS IN CHURCH Sunday morning. Aunts, uncles and cousins looked as if they'd put their two cents in, too, and Gramps was wryly noncommittal. Mother, from her seat in the choir, must have cased the situation, for when we gathered on the sidewalk after service she hissed, "Stay out of it. We don't need another civil war about the Hodges." Her eyes traveled over to Mrs. Hodge, large and blonde in her slightly-too-modish furs. Mr. Hodge wasn't with her, which was not surprising. Paul *was*. His blue eyes were sullen and rebellious beneath the leprechaun fringe of golden hair.

"What *is* it about the Hodges, anyway?"

"It's an old story. Nobody quite likes them, so everyone feels guilty, hence sorry for them. And the Hodges," Mother finished ironically, "don't quite like their son."

Gram was making her way, like a brisk determined bird, in the Hodge direction.

"DO YOU KNOW WHAT MAMA DID?" KATIE DEMANDED IN A rage, dragging me into a corner at Young Peoples that night. "Asked Paul flat out if he was going to be able to make the party! Said she hadn't heard and was worried his invitation might have miscarried in the mail!"

"What are you going to do?"

"What can I do? Tell him flat-out my mother is a liar?"

On Saturday morning a snowstorm hit, and there was a good deal of panic over the telephone wires until the snow tapered off in late afternoon. Gram recruited everyone to help with shoveling, and by seven-thirty, when I arrived, the threat to the festivities was past.

A burst of music greeted me—Melissa, her fingers

flashing up and down the piano keyboard. Our cousin, Leslie Skinner, who'd come down from Stamford on the train, was doing one of his grand opera baritone improvisations. None of the non-family guests had yet arrived. Katie's voice hollered for me from her bedroom, and I went upstairs, dragging my suitcase, for I planned to spend the night.

Katie looked sensational. Her hair was up with the Spanish comb, and the neckline of her red chiffon was all that Aunt Sadie had described. "I ripped out the net Mama sewed in," Katie said. "She hasn't seen my hair yet, either. I won't go downstairs till somebody gets here. Mama never bawls us out in front of people."

"She'll say plenty after."

"By then it will be too late. And it'll be worth it. It had better be," Katie said fervently. "Anyway, Mama's in a good mood. Look at this."

She held up a slender chain with a gold and amethyst drop.

"Pa gave it to her, a couple of centuries ago. I never thought she'd part with it; even Melissa couldn't pry it from her."

"She gave it to you?"

"Marched in here an hour ago and plunked it on the bureau, sounding angry. You know Mama," Katie said. " 'Seeing's you're getting so almighty grown-up and highfaluting, might as well have it. Tarnation stupid, something worth that much lying around hardly ever worn.' It'll clash like the dickens with my dress, but

I'm going to wear it. Oh, drat, my hair's falling down. Fix it for me, will you, before I put that thing on?"

She laid the pendant on the bureau as I made the necessary repairs.

There was stamping on the front porch, and the doorbell rang. "Katie Allison!" Gram hollered. "Tarnation get yourself down here, everyone's arriving!"

We ran downstairs, and Gram looked volumes at the altered neckline but her lips stayed sealed. Katie just let her stew and concentrated on the guests. Most of the leading lights of school were there—the presidents of student government and the senior class, a cross-section of the prettiest, the brightest, the most fun. I began to understand why Katie had been so busy feeding out snippets of information about coming attractions. The Sterling house, that twenty-third of January, was decidedly "The Place To Be."

The parlor floor was polished, and Melissa at the keyboard alternated in attraction with Melissa teaching the steps to the latest dances. The dance programmes were a great success. And after the first few minutes of horseplay, we all were besieged with partners. Everybody looked different, special, with that particular party glow. Except Paul Hodge, of course, who looked as ratty as Katie had expected. But Katie was following Gram's excellent example and saving her sarcasm for later on.

I floated through the two-step, the lulu-fado and maxixe with a variety of partners that ought to have had me overjoyed. But over blue serge and grey flannel shoulders, past brown heads and black and sandy, I kept looking for particular dark-gold hair and teasing hazel eyes.

The house rocked with music and laughter and dancing feet, and the punch bowl was constantly refilled. Presently I stopped watching the door and began to have a very good time. My hair was falling down, and my face was flushed, and I was prancing through the maxixe with Tim Molloy when a hand tapped his shoulders, and a voice I'd have recognized if I heard it on the moon said, "May I have this dance, just so I know there's no hard feelings over the debate?"

For a minute I worried about my falling hair, then I just surrendered to the music, and Mark's body against mine, and his arms guiding me. When my next partner came to claim me, he murmured, "Get lost, bud," and swept me off again. It was absolute heaven. When the dance was over, Mark fetched me punch, and we stood sipping, smiling at each other. If I'm dreaming, I thought giddily, I don't want to ever wake.

And then a mocking voice said, "For a congressman's son and the pride of Browning Society, you really can be an uncouth oaf."

Katie was standing there, glowing with exhilaration, a throaty chuckle in her voice. She was looking straight at Mark, and after a moment's astonishment, his eyes narrowed with that familiar challenge.

"That's an interesting opening line, Miss Sterling. What's the follow-up?"

"For someone suave, you haven't once asked your hostess for a dance. What's the matter, afraid I can't keep up with you, or you with me?" Katie gave that laugh again. My throat felt dry, and my ears were ringing, but not so much that I couldn't hear Mark's amused, "We'll just have to find out, won't we?"

He swept her off. I was left standing by the punch bowl, with my eyes open at last.

Katie hadn't guessed my secret. Katie wanted Mark for herself. And she'd gotten him. I wasn't old enough, clever enough, mean enough to compete with her and win.

I wanted to run and hide, but in our family we don't do that. In a few minutes Tim Molloy came over and said, "All this terpsichorean stuff makes me thirsty. Let's go to the kitchen and see if we can find something bigger than these dinky cups," and so we did.

For a non-actress, I did a pretty good job of covering up for the next hour, kidding with Tim and my grandfather and Uncle Peter, who was out in the kitchen with his pet crow Iago on his shoulder. Iago was getting handouts and making naughty noises, to the counterpoint of Gram's habitual mutter that crows weren't house pets. We helped set the buffet in the dining room. Gram had done Katie proud. There were salads and her famous tea sandwiches, the crusts of which Tim and Iago had been devouring as fast as she sliced them off. Afterwards there was ice cream, and a cake blazing with candles, and hot chocolate. Katie did the expected with the candles, but other than that she was glued to Mark's side, or vice versa.

Gram, too, had noticed. Gram said, in a brook-no-

nonsense voice, "No more dancing; you young folks've had enough opportunity to make fools of yourselves like grown-ups. Time for one good mixing game afore I send you home."

Tim, with the usual devil in him, suggested Sardines.

There were ribald roars that left Gram baffled, for somehow it had escaped her attention that Sardines, a kind of Hide-and-Go-Seek in reverse, provides plenty of opportunities for what she did not have in mind. One person hides, everybody looks and, upon finding, squeezes into the hiding place, too. It leads to a lot of proximity, and other things besides. Gramp just laughed. "All right, you can use the whole house except attic and cellar, and no hiding outdoors. I don't want parents complaining tomorrow that you've caught your death."

After much catcalling Tim Molloy was stuck for being It. Everybody closed eyes, and he vanished while Gramp counted to a hundred.

I felt as if I'd already been It in a game I didn't understand well enough, and had failed. I couldn't go home, without my defection being noticed and discussed. The attic was taboo for the others because that's where the parlor furniture and a lot of the secretarial school records were stashed. But Gramp wouldn't mind if I went there; I was family. As soon as Gramp said "Ninety-nine, *One Hundred!*" and the mob dispersed, I sneaked out to the kitchen and opened the door to the back stairs. Gram and Aunt Marnie, immersed in dishes, didn't see me, but Paul Hodge did. He had his hand on the back door handle, and to my surprise he winked and put a finger to his lips conspiratorially before slipping out. He was going home, I thought, but when I reached the landing, I saw him through the window, leaning against a tree in the back yard, lighting a cigarette.

I crept up to the attic, not daring a lamp, and curled up on the old sofa to surrender to an orgy of self-pity. This was one of Aunt Tish's old hiding places, where she sought solitude to write in high school days; recollecting her suddenly made my own misery seem petty. Nonetheless, there was a constricting pain in my chest and a leaden feeling in my stomach.

After a while my fears ceased, but I sat on, feeling drained, hearing faintly the sounds of footsteps and laughter down below. The window beside me looked out on the back yard, and a shaft of gold light from the kitchen touched Paul, quiet beneath the icy tree. The glow of his cigarette was a tiny, companionable beacon in the dark.

A shout of excitement told me the game was over. "More punch and cookies, then you all go home!" Gram called. I wanted to stay hidden, but I didn't want my absence marked. I got up, stiff from the position into which I'd squeezed; went down to Katie's bedroom and repaired my hair and blotted my face with the powder Gram doesn't know she wears. When I went downstairs, everybody was in the kitchen, and Paul was just coming in through the back door.

Punch and cookies circulated. Gram looked at the clock, remarked pointedly that it now was morning, and threw everybody out. Katie stood at the front door, doing the gracious hostess routine. Mark was the last to go, and before he did he took her hand in both of his, and held it for a moment, looking deep into her eyes. We'd both seen Richard Barthlemess do that in a movie, and Katie'd laughed, but she wasn't laughing now. No more was I.

Then there was only family left, Katie in a daze, Gram and the aunts congratulating themselves on the party's success. Leslie dropped a chip of ice down Melissa's back, and she threw ice back at him. There was more stamping on the porch, and Junius and Stella burst in. "We got back from a dinner party and thought we'd come up for a gossip session. Happy Birthday, Katie. How's your loot?"

They handed over their birthday contribution, and Katie had to run through the list of all she had received.

Gram sniffed. "Might show 'em that amethyst gewgaw. *If* you remember it. Notice you didn't think enough of it to wear it."

Katie blushed. "I meant to! I was just putting it on when you called me down—I'm sorry, Mama. Wait, I'll go get it."

She flew up the stairs, but there was quite a wait before she reappeared, and when she did her face was pale. "It isn't there."

"What do you mean, not there?" Gram's nostrils flared. "Your fault, might have known you're not old enough to trust, got giddy in the head when you thought that fool Schuyler boy was coming and dropped it somewhere—"

"*Mama,*" Mother said sharply. "Calm down."

She did, and Katie who'd been about to explode at her did, too. We searched the folds of Katie's dress, thinking it might have fallen and been caught there. We all trooped upstairs to her room and examined the floor, the bureau.

"It was here," Katie said doggedly. "Swear to God. I was going to hook the clasp, and then my hair was falling, and I put it on the bureau to wait till after Saranne had fixed that for me. You remember." I nodded slowly.

"Well, it's gone," Stella said practically. "If she left it here, and it's not in the room, which we know because we've looked, there's only one explanation. It didn't walk off by itself."

There was a silence.

Something changed in Gram's eyes. "Hate to say this," she said heavily, "but there was only one person here tonight I wouldn't put this past."

*Paul Hodge.* The name hung in the air.

"I knew we shouldn't have him here," Katie said wildly. "You see, Mama? I *told* you he wasn't to be trusted."

"*You hush,*" Gram said fiercely. "Bad enough we're thinking what we are, without'n putting it in words. And God help me, I am thinking it. But we're not going to go round flinging accusations less'n we're sure.

Though land knows, there's been enough provocation." She bit off, abruptly, the explanation of what that meant. "Come back downstairs. Put the kettle on."

We went, and Uncle Ben made coffee, and we sat around the kitchen drinking it. It was almost like every other family get-together. But not quite.

"Want to come home with us after all?" Mother whispered to me as Dad fetched her furs. I shook my head.

I went upstairs with Katie and, both of us strangely silent, prepared for bed.

# III

SCHOOL WAS BUZZING ALL WEEK ABOUT KATIE'S PARTY. IT was also buzzing with the information that Katie Sterling and MSS III were an item. Not that you would necessarily know this from Mark's behavior, for he was too debonaire to walk a girl to and from classes, carrying her books. But there was a fascinated gleam in his eyes when he looked at her, a different note in the challenge of his voice. There was a new glow to Katie.

I teased Katie gaily along with all the others and rejoiced with her at appropriate moments; I had that much decency. Or pride. But it was hard seeing her light up when Mark was near; having too much time, in the quiet hours at home, to think and feel. I used to escape from that echoing vacuum to the cheerful bustle of Katie's house; I didn't want to, now.

I threw myself into schoolwork, which benefited my Latin if not my state of heart, and into Browning Society whenever I could do so without risking encounter with MSS III.

Browning Society met on Friday afternoon to consider the matter of Spring Show. This was a tradition dating back to Aunt Tish's time. There was the usual division of opinion: Serious play or funny?

"We're a *literary* society, remember? That means Something of Significant Worth."

Tim Molloy groaned. "My father gets depressed enough every time he reads the evening paper."

There was a momentary silence. Involuntarily, I remembered Aunt Tish. The words popped out. "We ought to do something to do with the War. It's what's on everybody's minds."

"We won't get in the War," Mark said. "Not if Wilson keeps his head. All the talk is just scare tactics. Teddy Roosevelt and his warmongers trying to get votes."

Katie opened her mouth, then shut it again.

"I take it everyone does want a play," Miss Olsen interjected. "I will have to choose it, since I'm responsible for casting and direction. But does anyone have something to suggest?"

Mark leaned back on his elbows and quirked his brows. *"Macbeth,"* he said.

A concerted groan. *"Heavy!"* "And not enough women's roles."

For a moment I could see Mark on the battlements of Dunsinane.

*"Julius Caesar,* then. That's also about war and a tyrant."

"Same complaint. I know we've got to live up to the Society's lofty reputation," Tim said plaintively, "but didn't Shakespeare write anything that could be *fun?"*

"I was thinking," Miss Olsen said casually, "of *Merchant of Venice.* You all read it in school, so you're familiar with it." There were exaggerated memories of misery, and she laughed. "It *is* a comedy, as you'd realize if you saw it played. And it has plenty of good women's roles. Crowd scenes. Beautiful costumes," she added artfully, "and lots of horseplay for the men."

Mark raised an eyebrow. "Do you really think it would be suitable?" he asked. "I agree we should do something that has some meat to it. But it seems to me we would be much better able to cast something that had a really powerful hero in it. Besides, we have no one to play Shylock."

That meant he didn't want to play it, I saw in a moment of clarity. He'd be a good Macbeth, or Mark Anthony. But he didn't want to be a shriveled old man.

I heard my own voice saying suddenly, "You know who could be good as Shylock? Paul Hodge."

You could have heard a feather drop, everyone was so stunned. I was, myself. Then Mark laughed shortly.

"Hodge isn't in Browning Society. And even if he were, he'd scarcely be a good risk, would he?"

"I think," Miss Olsen said, "it's time this meeting adjourned. I'll call another meeting in about a week."

"IT MAKES ME SO MAD!" I EXPLODED AT THE DINNER table. "I know Paul's wild, and I don't like him either, but it wasn't such a crazy idea. There have been people in the plays before who weren't Browning members; you told me so. But Mark kept acting as if I were really stupid."

"And it's just barely possible that he's also thinking about what play has the best role in it for him," Mother added drily.

This was so completely a mirror of what had occurred to me earlier that I felt guilty. "If Mark is—sure of himself, he's got good reason to be."

"I have noticed," Dad said wryly, "that he doesn't exactly like to share the spotlight. It doesn't seem to occur to either him or his father that other people have abilities to develop, too."

"But he really doesn't think Paul Hodge has them. And he may be right. After all, Paul certainly didn't have the grades to be invited into Browning Society."

But that hadn't really been what was bothering the kids this afternoon!

Mother has such a disconcerting way of being on my same train of thought. "Browning Society *has* been turning into a snob group again. It's a shame. As an old grad, perhaps I'd better have a little talk with Katrin

Olsen. She's fairly new at the school, she may not have noticed."

"Mother! Don't you dare!"

A WEEK LATER, MISS OLSEN ANNOUNCED THAT AFTER CON-ferring with Mr. Moore, she had decided that *The Merchant of Venice* would indeed be a good idea. "It's a splendid opportunity to show the whole school that Shakespeare can be fun. And it makes valuable points about mercy and compassion—and prejudice—of which we're all guilty from time to time."

"Well, of course." Mark's tone was faintly patronizing. "If you really think you'll be able to cast it, Miss Olsen. . . ."

"That's another thing," Miss Olsen said firmly. "Mr. Moore agrees with me that it is especially important, in this year of War, for all Americans not only to affirm but to demonstrate the principles of democracy. There is no reason why participation in the production should not be opened to the entire school, as I believe was the custom some years ago."

"HONESTLY!" KATIE SAID IN EXASPERATION, WALKING home. "Nobody in school will want to sit through a whole night of Shakespeare when they could go to the movies for ten cents instead."

"You won't think that way if you get Portia, which I assume you're trying out for," I said waspishly. Katie had the grace to blush.

FOR ALL THAT THE BRONX IS RAPIDLY BECOMING CITIFIED, its grapevine still operates with small town efficiency. Both Mother and Dad heard about the play before reaching home that evening, she from Altar Guild and he from his law office where he'd received a telephone call from Mr. Schuyler wondering if he didn't think Mr. Moore was exceeding his authority.

"I wish he'd go back to minding the State's business in Washington and let us alone," Dad added.

"Sidney!" Mother said sternly, her lips twitching.

"The Schuylers are right, for once. That wild Hodge boy doesn't belong in any activity with decent children." Aunt Sadie rose from the dinner table, fuming. "I have a good mind to march down to that school tomorrow and straighten out Charles Moore. I still have some influence in this town."

The front door opened and closed, and Gram walked in. She hadn't even rung the doorbell, which showed she was in a state; and without even taking off her coat or overshoes, she tramped across the Oriental rugs. They had belonged to Grandmother Albright; and Aunt Sadie, who doesn't much like Gram anyway, is very protective of them. "Bronwyn, put the kettle on," Gram ordered, unwinding her cocoon of coat and mufflers.

"Mama, what is it? Didn't you have night school tonight?"

"Your father still there. Stopping by here later. Couldn't stay any longer, so shook up I'm ready to explode and that fool man thinks I'm wrought up over nothing." Gram, unwrapped, plopped into the chair that Dad held out for her.

I had a sinking feeling. "Katie isn't getting a real mad on at me, is she?"

Gram stared blankly. "Katie? No. It's Melissa who's dropped the bombshell this time. Stopped by the school and just informed us casually. Right before I was due to give dictation; couldn't talk straight, made a fool of myself, your grandfather had to take over. I could kill that girl."

Mother shoved a cup of coffee before her. "Mama, what did Melissa tell you?"

"Tell is right. No asking permission, even for politeness sake."

*"Mama!"*

Gram took a long swig of coffee. "Melissa's getting married."

If she wanted to cause a sensation, she succeeded. We stared at her.

"But to whom?" Mother asked at last.

"You may well ask," Gram retorted grimly. "Considering the way she's been lallygagging with half the sheiks in town, was beginning to wonder if she was planning to set up a male harem. You all saw her at Katie's party, spreading her charm around. All an act, I suppose, to keep me from catching on!"

"Evie," Dad said mildly, "don't you think you might tell us who's the lucky man?"

"Leslie Skinner's who! Leslie, my sister Annie's boy, her own first cousin—"

"Now, Mama, you know they're not blood kin. Aunt Annie got both Leslie and Alice from the orphan asylum."

"Brought up as first cousins." Gram would not be dissuaded. "And not a peep from either of them that they were getting sweet on each other in that way. Oh, I suppose they're very proud of themselves, how they fooled us. Marched into the school office grinning like idiots, announced they'd just settled it and want to be married soon, on account of Leslie's in the National Guard, and he's got an idea we're going to land in the War real soon."

"What did Gramp say?" I asked, fascinated.

"Told them he agreed with them," Gram said acidly. "Can you believe it, they've taken the train to Stamford in this weather, to tell Will and Annie, and I can't even phone Annie to let off steam because I'd spoil their great announcement! So I took two aspirin and came here. Bronwyn, whether Melissa cottons to the idea or not, I'm having an announcement party week from Saturday, and you'll have to help."

It was lovely having Melissa's bombshell come just then. Gram, determined to do things up brown, was inviting everyone to the engagement party—favorite teachers as well as families of nearly all our crowd. The flurry competed for attention with Browning auditions the next week.

Auditions started at once and went not well. I heard this second-hand, for I did not attend. Katie read twice and came out fuming. "Don't ask! I don't want to talk about it!" she said when I tried to probe.

"What happened?" I demanded of Tim Molloy, when we had walked her home.

Tim grinned. "She read for Portia, and she wasn't bad, except she didn't like it when Miss Olsen told her Portia was not a supercilious know-it-all. You know how Katie always wants to have all the answers! And Mark read Bassanio, in much the same key, which flustered her—I wonder why!" He paused. "Mark also read Shylock."

"And?"

"He stank," Tim said bluntly. "He sounded like his old man, doling out grace-and-favor at the party office. Not Shylock by a country mile. And the worst of it is, we may have to be afflicted with it."

"You aren't serious?"

"Never more. The gossip is that Olsen finally got hold of Hodge when he showed up in English class for once, and he told her he didn't owe the school no blooming favors and they could keep their blooming condescension. Language cleaned up for your delicate ears. Anyway, sweetie, you'd better give Olsen some of your support and sympathy next time you see her. She's been asking why you haven't come to tryouts."

I felt like a heel, but not enough so to go to the auditions.

AT HOME, PLANS FOR THE ENGAGEMENT PARTY WERE BURgeoning. Gram was getting on everyone's nerves.

Katie telephoned one afternoon late in the week. "Come and eat dinner with me, won't you, and stay over? Everybody's out." She sounded subdued. I went up, and we concocted an exotic recipe out of leftovers and ate in the kitchen.

"We don't dare make a mess in the rest of the house or Ma'll skin me," Katie warned. "There's no living with her till the party's over. Right now she's blaming everyone else because she got herself into it."

The house was spit-and-polish bright, and very silent. It occurred to me that being the youngest, even in a large family, could be as lonely as being an only child. Especially if both one's parents went out to business. Katie, in an old bathrobe, with her hair down, sounded forlorn.

"How is everything?" I inquired delicately.

Katie shrugged. "I don't know if I'm going to get Portia. I don't even know if I *want* her anymore." She pushed back her hair. "Oh, rats, I don't know if we're even going to be able to do the play."

That was as close as she'd come to mentioning the Paul Hodge–Shylock mess.

"I should think Mark would be wonderful as Bassanio."

"I don't know where anything stands in that direction either," Katie burst out suddenly. "I thought at my party. . . . Maybe I was just imagining things. He never walks me to class, or pays special attention, just lounges against the wall sounding sardonic. Mama says I should stop mooning, think of the poor girls growing up in France and England, and count my blessings. Fat lot that did to make me feel better, but she's probably right. I should give up."

A disloyal little worm of hope wriggled in my heart.

MISS OLSEN STOPPED ME ON THE WAY OUT OF ENGLISH class on Friday. "Saranne, could you stop by my classroom this afternoon?"

"I don't want to try out for the play."

"I didn't say anything about that, did I?" Miss Olsen countered. "I just want to speak to you for a few minutes. Please, Saranne."

It was the note in her voice when she said "Please" that did it.

I didn't get there right at three, having again been detained for a discussion of my Latin by Mr. Dirksen. Her door was closed, and she didn't hear right away when I opened it; she was sitting at her desk with her head on her hands above a pile of papers. I said, "Miss Olsen?" hesitantly, and she straightened quickly.

"Come in, dear. I was woolgathering." She smiled ruefully, but her voice was shaky.

"Miss Olsen, are you all right?"

"Just a bad day. Teachers have them, too, you know. And if Mark Schuyler asks me one more time how soon I'm going to announce the cast—!"

"Tryouts aren't going well, are they?" I asked impulsively.

"You've heard that, have you?" Miss Olsen looked at me sharply. "No, they're not. I'm beginning to wonder if I made the wrong decision." She hesitated. "I spoke to Paul Hodge, as you may have heard, but I got nowhere. I thought perhaps, since you'd made the suggestion, you might have some influence."

I stared at her, appalled. "I hardly know him!"

"But you did—see the possibility. Your family and the Hodges, I understand, have known each other for years. And your family has so much good influence in West Farms." Miss Olsen looked at me earnestly. "Saranne, I think it could be very important for Paul Hodge to be in this play. Not just so we can do it. I think he needs to be attracted into something worthwhile, before it's too late. There's so much anger in him. Everyone expects the worst, even before it happens, and he obliges. Just like Shylock. You saw that, didn't you?"

I didn't answer.

"I don't understand it," Miss Olsen said. "I don't need to know the reasons. But it tears me apart to see him throwing so much potential down the drain, and nobody lifting a finger to dissuade him. Just as I suspect you, in different ways, are throwing away potential."

"Miss Olsen," I said slowly, "I'll help you in any way I can—backstage, or taking notes, or helping you at rehearsals. But I won't get up on stage. And I can't, I just can't, talk to Paul."

THE HODGES WERE COMING TO THE ENGAGEMENT PARTY, Gram having boxed herself into that one by insisting on Paul's presence at Katie's birthday. The Schuylers were coming too, since Mark's father was still around strengthening political fences locally.

By the day of the party, Gramp was taking refuge with Dad in Dad's study. Everyone had given up trying to make Gram take it easy and was letting her just run her motor down. The February skies were lowering, but sleet held off till the Skinners arrived on the train from Stamford. Fortunately, the weather cleared by evening, although the streets were sheets of ice.

"Our Leslie this" and "our Leslie that," Gram kept saying, and you'd never know she'd carried on the way she had when Melissa broke the news.

There was Gram's usual lavish array of food. There were toasts and the announcement, which was no surprise, couched by Gramp in one of his famous poems. There were congratulations and music and dancing. Presently the party shook itself comfortably down into the usual categories. And the younger crowd took over the kitchen.

The boys and Iago devoured sandwich crusts as fast as Katie sliced them off, as usual, and in a very few minutes conversation had narrowed in on the play. Mark was talking earnestly about how it was his responsibility as President not to let Browning Society fail to live up to its high calling. Dedication, high literary and artistic and cultural and moral standards.

"Etc., etc., etc.," Katie whispered scathingly. She was upset because she was being ignored. "It's time he wrote a new speech."

They *were* the same sardonic words, but something

was different—a newer and more personal tone. And gradually I realized that though he was speaking to the crowd at large, his eyes were focused over all our heads towards one particular figure slouched by the door.

Not, as Katie was probably bitterly assuming, at a girl. At Paul Hodge.

If Miss Olsen had cornered Paul about the play, then Mark was proclaiming that Browning Society disavowed its faculty advisor's stance.

I felt Tim looking at me and knew he too understood. I wondered why Paul didn't walk out; why he'd come at all. Probably because his father was in the other room, and drinking.

I took a deep breath. "Why do we have to keep hashing this over?" I said loudly. "This is a party, for heaven's sake! Why don't we go inside and dance?"

"Because it's time we all were getting home," somebody's mother said firmly from the hallway. "It's started sleeting again." That started a general exodus towards boots and wraps. Pretty soon most of the crowd was gone. Mr. Schuyler was still trying to convince Dad that America wasn't going to get into the War, and Mrs. Hodge was trying ineffectually to get her husband to his feet. I started helping Mother and Gram clear the table.

I walked into the kitchen, intent on not spilling the punch bowl, and stopped dead. Mark and Katie and Paul Hodge were still there, and open war had broken out.

". . . hell of a lot you care about your precious Society!" Paul was shouting. "If you did, you'd be standing behind it, not sniping at everything that lady's trying to do to get that stupid play produced."

Paul was no fool, my mind registered dazedly.

". . . no position to talk about *my* support," Mark said hotly. "Not when you were practically begged to do something decent for the school for once, redeem yourself a little, and you throw the opportunity in 'that lady's' face!"

"*Redeem* myself? In *your* eyes? Why the blazing hell should I do you a favor and help out your snob club?" Paul's fists were clenched, and he was breathing hard. "No wonder you're so sure we won't get in the War; you sound like one of the Kaiser's Prussian officers yourself!"

Mark's face turned color. He took a step forward. Paul's fists came up. And suddenly Katie's voice was bursting out in a frenzy.

"How *dare* you accuse Mark of a thing like that! You aren't fit to—if he doesn't want untrustworthy riff-raff in Browning activities, is it any wonder? How do you expect any of us to want you, after you stole Mama's lavaliere from my room the night of my birthday party?"

There was an appalling stillness, then two voices came at once.

"*But I never—*" Paul said in absolute bewilderment.

"*Katherine!*" Gram said from behind me in a terrible voice.

My legs felt weak. The punch bowl, forgotten, slid from my arms and crashed to the floor in a thousand pieces, the tea-colored liquid splashing onto my blue georgette dress. There was another awful stillness. I stared at the floor, half-hypnotized, as the light from the hanging lamp was refracted off the shattered glass. Red; gold; unwinking; like the glow of Paul's cigarette that had somehow comforted me while I licked my wounds in the attic on Katie's birthday night.

"I don't know what the hell you're talking about," Paul said to Katie in a very quiet voice.

"Yes, you do." She sounded shaky, as she always did after a temper outburst, but she spoke with absolute conviction. "Mama gave me her amethyst lavaliere for my birthday. I never got to put it on. It was on my bureau, and it was still there when we started to play *Sardines,* I remember I saw it then. It was gone right after. Somebody took it while we were hiding, and you're the only one who could have."

She meant *would have,* and everybody knew it. Everybody agreed. I even saw it in Mrs. Hodge's face—the grownups having heard the crash and come flocking in. Paul stiffened, on the verge of an explosion. Then the life went out of him.

"What the hell's the use. You made up your minds about me a long time ago."

I stared at the broken glass, and something clicked in my mind.

"Oh, come, old man," Mark was saying. "You know Katie's not making all that up. Why don't you make things easier on yourself and admit you did it?"

"But he couldn't have," my voice said mechanically.

"He couldn't have. Because the lavaliere didn't disappear till during the Sardines game, and he was outside smoking a cigarette all that time. I saw him go out, I saw him through the windows as I went up to the attic, and all the time I was there, and as I came down again. He didn't come in till we were in the kitchen, and he was there with us until he left the party."

Everyone was looking at me, Paul most of all.

"It's very brave of you to stand up for him, Saranne," Mark said gently. "I know you wouldn't say that if you weren't absolutely sure that it was true. But are you *certain* you saw him every minute? That there couldn't have been the briefest time you didn't, and your mind's playing tricks telling you no one could have got in and out of the house so fast?"

For a moment, God help me, I was tempted. Because Mark was looking at me with that expression of peculiar intimacy.

Katie hadn't hooked him. I still had a chance. I knew that, just as I knew that if I persisted now I'd be cutting my throat forever.

"I'm not mistaken," I said doggedly. "I know what I saw. Paul didn't do it."

# March

# IV

THE ONLY WAY TO SALVAGE THE SITUATION WAS THROUGH form alone. The family came through magnificently, which was fortunate, because neither Katie nor I were up to it. Mark and Paul were stunned. I would have taken ironic pleasure in that if I hadn't been so stunned myself. But Gramp in his matter-of-fact way was saying, "Mark, your mother's waiting for you to help her down the steps, they're pretty icy." Mother, equally calm, turned to Paul.

"I think you'd better see if you can get your father up. He's in the den, and he's under the weather."

Mr. Hodge, thank God, having reached the sheep-drunk stage, hadn't heard what was going on. For an instant, I didn't think Paul was going to obey. Then, just as earlier, something alive in him seemed to die, and he pushed past us in silence.

Gram touched Mrs. Hodge's arm. "Hadn't you better go along too, Grace Alice? I'll see you tomorrow."

Gramp eased everyone toward the front door.

Katie and I were trapped in the kitchen by Gram's eyes, which had us impaled like butterflies on pins. "Well?" she asked ominously.

Katie burst into angry tears. "Don't you dare light into me, Mama! I just did what everybody else has been too chicken to do, and you know it!"

"Chicken's one thing, common sense is another," Gram snapped. "Not to mention kindness. You proud of yourself, young lady, ruining your sister's engagement party, blackening the name of a family that's already had plenty to contend with? Neighbors, go to the same church, poor Grace Alice—"

" 'Poor Grace Alice,' " Katie broke in hotly, "doesn't care two cents about Paul's reputation and you know it! What was I supposed to do, Mama, let Paul say those unfair things about Mark? You think a fight would have helped the party any? You want Paul to get away with your lavaliere, when we know he has it?"

" 'Knowing' something and being able to prove it are two different things," Gram retorted, "as you just found out. As for you, Saranne, seems to me you could've spoken sooner, soon's we started having those suspicions, would have saved us all a peck of trouble."

All I could say, miserably, was, "I didn't think of it till now."

"We've all said too much," Mother said briskly, "and we're all dead tired. Mama, unless you need any further help, Sidney and Saranne and I will go."

Gram shook her head. She didn't trust herself to

speak, and neither, fortunately, did Katie, but her eyes were absolutely furious.

The grandfather clock in the hall was chiming two as I sat down to pull on my overshoes.

Hard on top of it, the doorbell shrilled.

For a moment everybody grew stiff, as people will when such sound comes in the middle of the night. Then Gram shook herself.

"Somebody forgot something. Don't know why they couldn't wait till morning." She opened the door and a messenger stood there, ice clotting his coat and cap grotesquely.

"Is this the Sterling residence?"

Gramp stepped forward. "Yes, it is," he said, and the boy said, "Overseas cable, and it's marked urgent."

"My God. Tish," Gram said faintly. Mother took her hand. Gramp signed the boy's pad and tipped him and shut the door behind him before slitting the envelope meticulously. Melissa and Leslie had disentangled themselves and were there, too. Katie looked scared.

It wasn't Tish, not in the way Gram meant, but it was bad.

> Anthony killed in action. Nichola and I coming U.S. first available ship.
> Letitia Maitland-Mayne

"Oh, my poor baby," Gram whispered.

"At least," Gramp said heavily, "they'll be here. They won't be in a war zone."

None of us mentioned the way ships were being sunk by German submarines.

"I'll speak to Schuyler," Dad said briskly. "Shipping schedules aren't being posted anymore, but he may be able to get some information in Washington. We'll talk about it after church tomorrow, Ed."

Dad and Mother and I walked down the icy hill together, huddled close.

Mother must have spoken to Mr. Derbyshire in the robing room, because when the ritual reached the point of his reciting the prayer "in time of war or tumult," which he had been using regularly this winter, he included, "We pray especially for our daughter Letitia Sterling Maitland-Mayne in her bereavement." Everyone swarmed around us after service. It was hard to keep repeating over and over the bare bones that were all we knew so far. It was hard having nearly everyone mention the danger of submarines during transatlantic crossings.

A tall blond man came pushing through the crowd.

"You know who that is?" Katie hissed. "That's Mr. Latham who showed up at the debate. He and Tish were sweet on each other once."

Mr. Latham moved through the ring of neighbors as if they were so many mosquitoes and went straight to Gram. "I'm coming over this afternoon, if I may. I have connections with some of the overseas wire services. I'll see if I can get you more information. And now, I have my automobile here. Can't I drive you and Mr. Sterling home?"

Gram only said, "Much obliged," but she clung to his arm as if it were the Rock of Gibraltar.

"Well!" Mother said, looking after them as they departed. "His coming back to New York just now could be a Godsend."

"What do you mean?"

"Oh, nothing," she said vaguely.

AUNT SADIE WAS RANKLED THAT SHE'D HEARD THE NEWS for the first time in church, none of us having remembered to tell her at the breakfast table. Her reaction was terse. "What the girl gets, marrying a foreigner, going off to live among a pack of heathen. Comes running back now, and I suppose you'll fall all over yourselves trying to make it up to her when she's only herself to blame."

Mother's lips pressed together in a thin straight line.

IN SCHOOL ON MONDAY, IT WAS THE SAME, FOR MR. MOORE and many of the teachers knew Aunt Tish. Katie and I kept saying, "Yes, it's awful," and, "No, we don't know when," until we wanted to scream. By lunchtime the subject had percolated down to the kids, and it sickened me that most of them found it romantic and exciting. Mother was right, we really didn't understand yet what war was.

"As Mark says," Katie said too staunchly, "most of the reports are exaggerations to sell papers."

" 'Mark says, Mark says.' Is he the congressman that he knows so much? I'm sick of what Mark says." We were on our way home from school at last, and I had had enough.

Katie looked at me. "What's the matter with you lately that you're so against him? It's not like you to be so unfair."

"I'm not."

"Hogwash! Look at the scene you created Saturday night!"

"The scene *I* created!"

"You certainly did." Katie's face was red. "If I didn't know you, I'd say it was sour grapes, or maiden scorned. We had Paul Hodge dead to rights, and you stood up for him for no other reason than to make Mark and me look bad."

"Katie, he didn't take your necklace."

"What if he didn't?" Katie said bluntly. "He couldn't prove it. All the other things we said about him *were* true. He's *dangerous,* Saranne. He needs to be—kept out of the way of harming people. But there's never been any way to stop him. There could have been, this time, if you'd kept quiet."

I just looked at her. "I don't believe this. You mean I should let him get framed for something he didn't do, because he really deserves the punishment for other things? Katie Allison Sterling, I never thought you could be so immoral!"

"It's not immoral—"

"Or maybe it's not a question of morality and justice at all. Maybe it's just a question of what Mark Schuyler wants, Mark Schuyler has to get, so he'll appreciate you!"

For a moment I thought she was going to hit me. She didn't; she whirled, knocking me by accident into a snowdrift, and without waiting to pull me out was off in a stumbling run down Tremont Street. I was left among my scattered books in indignity and a deep cold desolation.

A figure loomed beside me and a hand, roughened by ice and wind, reached to pull me out. I didn't see at first that it was Paul Hodge. He gathered my books and handed them to me, and I mumbled, "Thanks," incoherently. There was an awkward pause.

"She looked pretty mad. I hope it wasn't on account of—you know."

I turned scarlet. "It doesn't matter." I wished he'd leave; I didn't know how to start out gracefully, and I didn't want him walking beside me. But he hesitated.

"Saranne—thanks. For the other night. It took guts to say what you did. I wouldn't have expected it. Of anybody."

"I just told the truth."

"Most people wouldn't have." His voice wasn't bitter, just flat, as though he were stating a well-known fact; that was what shook me.

"Maybe you're pre-judging them as much as they do you." Miss Olsen's comment about the play being more important for Paul than vice versa rang in my ears. "Why should you just assume no one trusts you with anything, when you know darn well that people want you in the play."

"Damn few."

"But there still *are* a few, and you'd be good in it.

Only you won't do it, just because you're too proud to risk looking as if you're trying to prove yourself. You'd rather wallow in being an outlaw." I looked at his closed, sullen face and burst out angrily, "Oh, what's the use? You and Katie are two of a kind, you're so stubborn you'd cut off your nose to spite your face!"

I couldn't believe what was getting into me these days.

FEBRUARY SHIVERED INTO MARCH. DAD CAME HOME, HIS face grey, with a paper reporting the Germans' policy of unrestricted submarine warfare on the high seas. We still hadn't heard anything more about Aunt Tish. Katie had a kimono party one night; six of us stayed over and made fudge. We were supposedly studying for Latin exam, but we mostly talked about *The Merchant of Venice,* which was beginning to look like a lost cause. Or, rather, Abby and the others gossiped like mad, while Katie and I preserved a precarious silence.

The next day, as I emerged from the exams, Katie was waiting, overlooking the fact that she wasn't speaking to me. "The play's on again. Olsen's asked me to stop by after school and read once more." And the following morning the notice was up.

### !!!CAST LIST FOR BROWNING SOCIETY SPRING SHOW!!!

Katie got Portia.

Katie was Portia; Bassanio, predictably, was Mark,

and Shylock was Paul Hodge. I had to read the sign three times before I could trust my eyesight. Miss Olsen had gotten through to him after all.

Miss Olsen caught me in the hall on my way to lunch. "Thank you for changing your mind."

I just gaped at her.

"I gather you did use your power of persuasion after all."

It took me a moment to realize what she meant. Then I turned red. "I didn't talk Paul Hodge into anything. I thought you had."

"That's not what Paul says. He said you made him see things from an angle he hadn't thought of before."

I was glad Katie was not around to hear, or Mark. "I didn't do anything," I repeated.

"Anyway, thanks to you, he has decided to 'give the old guy a try,'" Miss Olsen said drily. "His words. And I hope you meant what you said about helping any way that wasn't onstage, because I want you to be my general assistant and notetaker. This play is going to be a handful, and you might say you got me into it."

She had me well and truly tied, I reflected ruefully, heading at last for lunch. Katie was surrounded by well-wishers, so I was spared her gloomy predictions about Paul Hodge, but I got them later as we walked home.

THE ATMOSPHERE CRACKLED AT THE FIRST REHEARSAL, setting the tone for all the ones to follow. I had no experience with plays, so I could not tell what was making things go so wrong. But something was—you could smell antagonism in the air. It was Paul Hodge, of course, but it was more than Paul. Perhaps it was Mark, who conducted himself just as he did when leading a Browning meeting . . . except that there he was President, and Miss Olsen only faculty advisor; here she was director and supposed to be in charge. Tim was Gratiano, Bassanio's friend, and Tim and Gratiano both were clowns. That made things fun, but it didn't help get things done. Aside from Katie, Mark, Paul and Tim, cast members were upperclassmen whom I scarcely knew. As for Katie, I could have shaken her—Katie sailed in with the well-known Sterling chips on both her shoulders, braced for trouble. And Paul showed up late.

Aside from Katie, Mark, Paul and Tim, cast members were upperclassmen whom I scarcely knew. I felt anomalous, sitting by Miss Olsen's side, loaning pencils to those who'd forgotten them, writing down blocking, keeping track of who'd been given what script. It was strange, seeing a play take form from this angle—or not take form.

After a week I began to understand. There was no center of gravity here—there were two energy forces, Mark and Paul, and everything else revolved in haphazard orbits.

The first time Paul read a scene, I saw jaws drop—but he lacked discipline. He did not write down directions in his script, he got to rehearsals late or not at all. He offered no excuse, was unapologetic. Mark had electricity, but something still was wrong. When I came home to dinner Friday with an uneasy expression on my face for the third time running, Mother looked at me and asked, surprisingly, "Is Mark a problem?"

"I don't understand. He reads so beautifully. He moves so beautifully, not to mention how he looks. All the time, I'm admiring how he speaks the words. And yet it's dead."

"Because he's trying to get you to admire. He's not trying to be Bassanio, or achieve Bassanio's goals. And you know what that makes all those fine speeches. 'A tale told by an idiot, full of sound and fury, signifying nothing.'" Mother nodded sagely. "I'll bet our Katie's not doing that."

"Nor Paul either. You should have heard them this afternoon, Mother. They were doing the trial scene, and it gave me goose bumps. Katie is so good. She almost made me cry, she was so baffled and angry, the way she gets, only it came out looking like Portia and not Katie. And then—when Paul as Shylock took out his knife to cut the pound of flesh and stropped it on his sole, Mark *laughed*. He apologized after to Miss Olsen, but when the scene started again he kept making comments underneath his breath. And yet when *he* was speaking, he was furious if anybody whispered, even though he really wasn't as good as Paul. He was always Mark, never Bassanio, especially in the scenes with Paul."

"I think," Dad said, "Miss Olsen has opened a can of worms."

"I think so, too. And I just hope it's not all my fault."

"Don't flatter yourself," Mother retorted drily. "Oh, Lord, Sidney, there's the doorbell and the dinner dishes still sitting on the table."

The caller was Congressman Schuyler. For a crazy instant I wondered if he'd come about the play and Paul Hodges, thinking I was responsible; then my sense of proportion, not to say sense of humor, righted itself. We hurried to the hall after my father, prudently closing the dining room doorway portieres behind us.

"Thank you, no, I won't sit down. I just got off the train from Washington. I wanted to get word to you and couldn't risk the telephone."

"From Washington?" Mother looked puzzled. Then she gasped. *"Tish?"*

Mr. Schuyler smiled. "I'm not allowed to reveal marine information in wartime, you understand. But a friend at a foreign embassy suggests you may want to be down to the docks tomorrow at dawn."

Dad was already striding toward the phone. "Don't say it on the wires!" Mr. Schuyler said sharply, and he called back, "Of course not. I'll tell Ed to call a gathering of the clan."


WE WERE UP ALL NIGHT, FOR AFTER GRAMP SUMMONED all our kin to their house, Gram made coffee and dug out a nut cake she'd whipped up after school, and we sat talking.

"Just got an itch telling me I needed something

on hand. Have to make another, though, if there's to be any for Tish and her young one."

Aunt Marnie laughed at her. "Mama, you know you love last-minute hustle!"

"Love it nothing. Last minute—good Lord o' thunder, it *is* last minute, spring cleaning not done, can't have that child coming into a pigsty."

She was working up a good head of steam, and the family burst into laughter, acknowledging the inevitable. We pitched into housecleaning, baking, polishing, fixing up Tish's old room for her and Nichola. By the time we finished, it was a quarter to four, and Gram said, "No use sleeping now," and made eggs and bacon. And then the sky was beginning to show streaks of light, and Dad and Junius and Uncle Ben brought round their autos, and we crammed in for the long ride to lower New York.

There had been excitement earlier; there was silence as we waited at the pier. Dad procured coffee somewhere. It was cold, here in the barnlike building with the open sides looking onto slips where ships could dock. Only a few lights burned.

"Probably trying not to tip the city off to a ship's arrival," my father said. But slowly, imperceptibly, the dock began to come to life. Stevedores arrived in twos and threes. A chestnut peddler. A few burly policemen, men wearing the insignia of the customs service, and two worried men in business suits and the badges of the steamship line.

Gram was standing somewhat apart, very upright,

her hat skewered firmly and her lips set in that no-nonsense expression that meant she was deeply moved. I went up and hugged her, and she patted my arm.

"Now don't set me hullaballooing, don't want to look like an old fool."

Behind us, other people had arrived. Like us, anonymous and subdued; like us, filled with anticipation and anxiety that communicated itself in a current too deep for words. Everyone was staring out toward the Narrows, toward the sea.

"Must be soon now," Dad whispered to my mother. "Odd, isn't it, how a crowd senses things?"

And sure enough, from very faint and far away, came a call. "Here she comes!"

Like one organism, the crowd surged toward the end of the pier.

Moving slowly, steadily up the ribbon of river, like a gallant grey old lady, came a steamer. She was battered, she was drab, she was nothing like the liners I'd read about in novels, and she was as the phrase went, "packed to the gunwales." That is if she had gunwales, and something told me that she did.

I couldn't swallow around the lump in my throat. I felt Katie, very close beside me, and suddenly she grabbed my hand and squeezed it.

By now the customs guards and policemen were pushing us all back behind ropes. The customs men went aboard.

"Where's Tish? I can't see Tish," Gram kept fuming as we waited.

She beat her hands together, moving like a tight-wound top. Gramp touched her arm, gently, and a look of extraordinary intimacy passed between them. I felt, at the same moment, a sense of warmth and belonging, and of almost palpable sadness.

My family. Here we all were—so close; so much alike; so different. What was this like for Aunt Tish, and for Nichola? (A cousin, she must be eight now, and English.) What was Aunt Tish like? (I scarcely remembered her.) "You're so much like her," Mother said to me sometimes with a decided dash of rue.

From time to time, guards let official-looking persons up or down the gangway. Then a murmur, faint at first, began to swell.

"They're taking the gate down," Dad said.

We were stampeded. The crowd swept us along toward another stream of figures pouring down the narrow, slat-sided ramp. I discovered that my heart was pounding. We were in the middle of a kaleidoscope not just of callers but of shouts, sobs, laughter. Dad, Gramp, Uncle Ben were tall enough to see above the crowd, and their eyes kept searching.

Gram's fist beat her hand. "Didn't come. Knew something would go wrong. All that cloak-and-dagger nonsense of Sherm Schuyler's, and she's not on board at all."

"Mama, calm down," Mother said automatically.

Then Gramp said, "Evie," in a firm and quiet voice, and Gram—all of us—looked where he pointed, through a gap that opened fortuitously. A woman was coming down the ramp, moving as through a fog, as though she were a part of the fog itself. She was dressed in grey, and her eyes were grey-dark, too, like those of the small girl pressed tightly to her side. Gram made a faint sound, and then she was scuttling like one of those harbor tugs, through the gap, through the ropes, past the guards, whose efforts to deter her she ignored. She went up to the woman, knelt for a moment by the little girl, then took them briskly by the hands and led them off.

Aunt Tish was home.

Aunt Tish and Nichola were home, and everything was anticlimactic. Everybody talked at once, but low-key and saying nothing—at least everybody but the travelers did. That was what dawned on me first, that they scarcely spoke at all. I was brought forward and presented, and a cool cheek pressed briefly against mine, a delicate scent of roses enveloped me. Nichola—blonde, pale, slight—suffered being hugged but was unresponsive. Aunt Marnie and Mother, and Katie even, were crying, Gram's eyes were bright. Aunt Tish's were dry, and dead, like someone who'd looked on everyone and everything and now saw nothing.

I wasn't seeing through a kaleidoscope now; more like through a camera lens that focused on a picture that was strangely skewed. Then my youngest cousins started wailing they were hungry, and Gram came to life. "What're we wasting time standing for, go home for breakfast, must all be starved. Guess you'll be glad to get back to no shortages," she said in Aunt Tish's direction. Aunt Tish didn't answer.

UNCLE BEN AND DAD WENT OFF TO SEE AUNT TISH'S LUG-gage through customs.

"Sidney's brought the car," Mother said. "We'd better move along." She steered Aunt Tish and Nichola toward the exit.

I don't know what I'd expected, but as our entourage rolled back toward the Bronx we all were silent. Gramp pointed out famous landmarks to Nichola, but got only a polite, "Yes, sir" in response. Her eyes, it seemed to me, looked dead. Neither she nor Aunt Tish spoke except when spoken to, and then only briefly.

Mother turned around in the front seat. "Look, Tish, the trees are budding in Central Park." Aunt Tish merely nodded.

The sun was golden, the morning was unfolding with the beauty of early spring, and I was even missing Latin class. But there were no banners flying, no sparklers bursting in midair. I hadn't expected them exactly, not with the War and my unknown Uncle Anthony's tragic death. But this was a reunion, a homecoming, so eagerly, so intensely looked forward to—and something wasn't there.

It was almost as though some*one* wasn't there. As though the physical forms of Aunt Tish and Nichola, whom we had welcomed, were only empty shells. The woman I was supposed to resemble simply was not there.

# V

IF EYES ARE WINDOWS TO THE SOUL, THEN AUNT TISH'S were like opaque grey shades where windows ought to be. The only time I saw the mists part for a moment was when we drew up at the house. Aunt Tish's hands tightened briefly. "It feels so strange. Nothing's changed."

"Oh, there are changes." Mother chuckled. "There's a gas stove now. Pa's talking about electric lighting, and an auto. Pa has three cats, and Peter has a crow."

"Aunt Kate's gone." Aunt Tish shook her head faintly. "How afraid of her we were. And yet, since the War started, I've found myself thinking, 'What would Aunt Kate do?' And it got me through."

"We've another Kate who's becoming alarmingly like her."

"And Miss Sadie?"

"Getting old. She lives with us now, you know," Mother said brightly.

We went in, acting unlike ourselves, our voices muted. I looked at Katie, and she rolled her eyes. Then Iago, who had been helping himself to the fruit that Gram had rashly set out in the dining room, came sailing in with raucous comments and broke the spell.

"It's good some things never change." Aunt Tish seemed not to know whether to laugh or cry. "Nikki, darling, it's all right, he's one of Uncle Peter's pets, like the snake I told you about, remember?" Nichola shrank back as Iago sidled up, and Tish shook her head. "Come along, dear, Mummy will help you wash up and then we'll have breakfast."

"Making pancakes in your honor," Gram called out as they went upstairs.

Nichola didn't like the pancakes. She didn't say so; she took two polite bites and pushed them to one side. "Please, I always have milky tea," she murmured when Gram offered her a glass of milk. Gram looked baffled.

"Good thing spring's coming. Do her good to get out and roughhouse with the younguns."

But Aunt Marnie's free-spirited brood, who had come in after we arrived, were staring at Nichola as if she were a visitor from another planet. She could well have been, she was so polite, contained, reserved.

"Glad to see you're not putting her in black. Ridiculous on a child," Gram looked pointedly at Aunt Tish's own mist-pale coat and skirt. For an instant, defensiveness flickered on Tish's face. Then it died.

"Anthony hated mourning."

A little undercurrent ran around the table. The subject had been broached.

Gramp cleared his throat. "Tish, what did happen? Your cable told us nothing."

"Not now, Pa." Aunt Tish's voice was very quiet. I saw the quick, alarmed glance she shot in Nichola's direction, but Gram did not.

"No use putting your head in the sand. Sooner you

get used to talking about it the better. The man's dead, Tish, and you got to face it."

"Mama, I said *not now*."

Nichola had gotten so rigid she was shaking. Her eyes were like black pools, but her small voice was steady. "Please, may I be excused to take a nap?"

"I'll take you," I murmured, but Gram realizing too late what she'd wrought, said, "*I* will."

"Please, I prefer my mummy." She wasn't rude, she was simply stating a fact. She went soberly off at Tish's side, leaving us all looking at one another.

"It ain't going to be easy," Aunt Marnie said profoundly.

"PLEASE, ALL OF YOU, GIVE HER TIME," AUNT TISH SAID when she came back down. "Don't push her. And don't mention the War or England, or—her father, unless she does. I mean it, Mama. We were bombed in a zeppelin raid, and ever since then Nichola's had the most dreadful nightmares. The doctors thought perhaps, if I got her away from London. . . . She adored her father. When he crashed—she can't accept it, not yet, there's been too much at once."

"Was he shot down?" Mother asked gently. Aunt Tish nodded. "He was shot down over occupied France on the eleventh of January."

A prickle ran down my spine.

The telephone rang. Gramp went to answer it. As soon as he started back, it rang again. This time, after hanging up, he took the receiver off the hook and came back, looking sober.

"Newspaper reporters. They saw your name on the passenger list and want interviews. I told them no, but they'll probably be calling back."

Aunt Tish straightened. For the first time I saw a resemblance to my mother. "I had better write a statement you can give them. May I use your desk, Pa?" She went into the study, her head high.

"We'd better get to school," Katie said. "Make sure the school hasn't been burned up in our absence."

I didn't like her choice of metaphors.

My thoughts were with Aunt Tish all day; when I went into rehearsal, I felt as though I were watching everything through a pane of glass. Perhaps that's why, as I ran around at my tasks, I sounded curt and bossy. Katie raised her eyebrows, and Tim murmured, "My, my, the Sterling temper emerging in such a nice little girl." I could have smacked him.

AT HOME, THE NETWORK BETWEEN OUR VARIOUS FAMILY houses sprang to life. Everybody was on the telephone that evening—talking *to* Aunt Tish, talking *about* Aunt Tish, offering advice. It occurred to me that Aunt Tish, like Nichola, needed to be given time. How long—two months since Uncle Anthony died?

In bits and pieces the story of those months—and the War years preceding them—emerged. The August Bank Holiday Monday when War had been declared, she and Anthony had walked the streets of London all that night, had cheered the king and queen on the balcony of Buckingham Palace. By nightfall Tuesday Anthony had been in uniform. "They all went," Aunt Tish said, stitching away quietly on one of Nichola's dresses as Mother and I drank tea with her one afternoon. "All our friends held commissions in one of the services. It was the thing. Some families have lost two sons, three. . . ."

Another time, in response to Katie's question, "I was working on a novel that summer, but I stopped. The theme seemed too trivial. Somehow, War's not a time for private issues. Anyway, since then, somehow, I haven't written."

Stella and Aunt Marnie tried, unsuccessfully, to make Nichola feel at home playing with their children. "Face it, Tish, that child has problems," Aunt Marnie said bluntly.

Aunt Tish just looked at her. "You think I don't know it? I'd hoped a change of scene might make it easier; it sometimes does. But it all had to happen so fast. The Government wanted to use our London house, passage was difficult, and we had to sail on a day's warning." She shuddered. "Six to a stateroom, the men slept on deck, no lights at night because of the threat of submarines. Is it any *wonder?*"

Aunt Tish had enrolled Nichola in school; Aunt Marnie's boys escorted her, and she went dutifully, but she hated it, and when she was at Gram's she spent most of her time up in her room. She started getting headaches, which had the whole family worried. And amid all this, there was old Dirksen, in school, and Mark, still saying it was not *our* war. And Paul, growing angrier by the minute.

"It's funny, in a way, that Paul's so anti-German," Katie said once, carelessly; "didn't there used to be a story they'd changed their name from Hartz?" and Mark heard her. After that I heard him, once or twice, refer to Paul as Hartz, or call Shylock "our *Deutsche* Jew." It was only teasing, the faintest flicking of a whip, but Paul's face grew taut.

It was becoming apparent, even to me, that Miss Olsen couldn't keep things like that, or rehearsal itself, under control. I hated acknowledging it, because I liked her. But Aunt Tish's return had prompted in Mother and Aunt Marnie streams of reminiscences of Browning Society in "the old days," when things had been very different.

"Even when we had Mary Lou Hodge and Ken Latham's older brother involved in plays, somehow things seemed to pull together," Aunt Marnie said. "Remember, Tish?"

"I remember," Aunt Tish said shortly. "It's better to let the past stay buried."

Mother shook her head. "Lightning used to strike, sometimes, in those days."

I was only too afraid of it striking, disastrously, now. And there came at last a rehearsal when I understood what she meant.

It started badly. Paul didn't show up, and I was sent searching him. Then Katie and Tim started clowning and were with difficulty brought back to business, Katie angry because *she'd* been ready to work when no one else was. One of the minor characters began Act III by asking, "Now, what news on the Rialto?"

From the back came a stage whisper. "Hodge is late again. That's *news?*"

The antagonism in the room crackled. And then Paul began it, the speech I had been thinking of when I'd blurted out his name, so unexpectedly, for the Shylock role.

> He hath disgraced me . . . laughed at my losses, mocked at my gains, scorned my nation, thwarted my bargains, cooled my friends, heated mine enemies—and what's his reason? I am a Jew. Hath not a Jew eyes? Hath not a Jew hands, organs, dimensions, senses, affections, passions? fed with the same food, hurt with the same weapons, subject to the same diseases, healed by the same means, warmed and cooled by the same winter and summer as a Christian is? If you prick us, do we not bleed? If you tickle us, do we not laugh? If you poison us, do we not die? And if you wrong us, shall we not revenge?

His voice shivered out into a silence that caught and held. For those moments, we were in Venice, in West Farms, in every place where persecution and prejudice shaped men's souls.

Then, from the back of the room, derisive and audible, came an imitation of a fire bell changing. From whom it came I did not know; don't ever want to know. Paul wheeled around, an exact image of himself as he had stood motionless that day of the fire. Then he bolted out.

Miss Olsen could not get rehearsal back under control and dismissed it.

I didn't wait for Katie. When I reached home the house was still. I went to the kitchen and started dinner preparations, but my mind refused to be soothed by the monotony of routine.

I was glad when the doorbell rang.

Not only did it ring, the doorknob rattled, and a hand was beating frantically against the wood. "Bron? Miss Sadie! Dear God, isn't anybody home?"

I threw the door open, and Aunt Tish half-fell inside, an Aunt Tish I had never seen. Her hair scraggled down around her haggard face, and she'd been crying. "Saranne . . . oh, thank God, I've been phoning everywhere, and no one's home. I don't know what to do . . ."

"Mother and Aunt Sadie are at suffrage meeting. Aunt Tish, what is it? Come sit down." I tried to steer her to the parlor, but she struck at me to get free.

"You don't understand. We have to find Nichola. She's gone."

I must have stared at her. Aunt Tish swallowed, and her eyes closed, her hands knotting until she got her voice under dry control.

"I was lying down. Nikki wasn't in school; she

wouldn't go; she said she was sick, but that was just excuse. She was in our room, in the window seat, just sitting. I must have drifted off . . . when I awoke, everything was still . . . there was no one there at all. . . ."

"Gram's at school. But Katie should be home by now."

"I don't know. I went out looking; haven't been back. I phoned all of you, and I couldn't get anyone, and I've just been looking—"

"Nichola's probably just gone out for a walk."

"*You don't understand.*" Aunt Tish's fists drummed against her legs. "Nichola's not—right about things, since Anthony . . . She won't talk about it, she won't say a word, but she didn't want to come here, she wants to go *Home.*"

I didn't understand, but I could feel the panic communicate itself to me. Aunt Tish's face looked bloodless, and she was shaking. "Sit down," I said sharply, and when she did, I put the kettle on the gas with one hand and reached for the telephone with the other.

Katie, thank God, was home. I filled her in quickly. "Call Tim and the other kids. And Mark—he's so proud of his executive skills, he might as well use them," I said brutally. "If you divide up the neighborhood into sections and get the school crowd searching, they should find her. They'd know where little kids are apt to go."

"OK. But don't panic. Look at all the times Missy and I wandered off when we were little."

"This is different." I dared not say more, for fear

Aunt Tish would hear. Katie drew her breath sharply.

"Saranne, you don't think the drainage ditch—?"

"I don't know! You run over there, you live nearer. I'll give Aunt Tish tea and then walk her back in case Nichola reappears."

I hung up; cranked the phone again. Junius's office. He would come join the search after alerting Dad and Stella. Ben's office. At last I got Aunt Marnie. She grasped the situation instantly.

"I'll get Bron out of the meeting, and call Pa and Mama. Jimmie's too far away, I guess. Saranne, stay calm. The last thing Tish needs is for us to get frantic, too."

I didn't know what she needed; I felt inadequate and helpless and when I went back into the parlor with the steaming teacup Aunt Tish was sitting like a statue carved from stone. The tears were running down her face, but they made no more impression than rain on marble.

I did the only thing I could; put the cup on a table and knelt down and wrapped my arms around her. But the shoulders that shook were mine.

After a moment she disengaged herself gently. "You remind me of someone. I think it's me."

"Gram said that once."

Aunt Tish smiled faintly. "Saranne, I understand what you're feeling, and I do appreciate, but don't bother. It doesn't make a bit of difference. I learned that, finally; I'm too afraid Nichola has, as well."

It was obscene that there was nothing at all that I

could do or say. We just sat there, and I built a fire, and Aunt Tish sipped her tea, and I fetched mine, glad to bury my face in its concealing steam. But pictures rose in the mists. Nichola with her faraway stare wandering through the streets of West Farms, heedless of motorcars, of the fact that traffic here moved to the right. Nichola, wanting to go Home. The few bare facts Tish had told us, and a plane going down in an orange cartwheel of flame.

"Nannie used to read the tea leaves," Aunt Tish said vaguely. "She was Anthony's nannie, and Nichola's too. From the Border counties, built like a Bath bun, with black currant eyes. And pleated caps with starched streamers. She read Anthony's cup the afternoon before he left and wouldn't tell us what she saw. Only begged him not to go. After that she wouldn't look into the cups at all."

*Her* eyes were dry as she gazed into the fire, but I wondered what she was seeing. Abruptly she set down her cup and rose.

"I can't sit here. I have to *do* something."

"Hadn't we better go back to Gram's?"

She nodded and followed me. In the street we passed Tim moving purposefully along. He saluted, but his eyes never stopped their surveyal of the yards. So the neighborhood militia had been mobilized.

Aunt Tish stopped suddenly like a startled animal. "That empty lot we used to play in . . . is it still there? There used to be a drainpipe children hid in."

"They still do. Katie will check it. Aunt Tish, you'd really better get on to the house." I spoke hurriedly, for I was remembering not just the pipe but the pond beyond, and the drainage ditch.

I kept Aunt Tish moving doggedly, kept trying not to see the pictures that formed behind my eyes. We got to Gram's house, and it was dark and empty. The clock was striking—a quarter to five. It seemed much later.

Dusk was falling. I lit some lamps. Aunt Tish hung up our coats; looked in the closet; said, "Well, at least she remembered to put on her overshoes," and gave a queer little laugh.

The phone rang, and it was Gram, wanting to know if we'd had any word. "Your grandfather phoned the police. No use wasting time." Matter-of-fact, as she always was in crisis. The phone rang again, and it was Aunt Marnie.

"Does Tish want me to come up? I can leave the kids with the neighbor."

Aunt Tish shook her head tightly.

The phone rang again, this time Junius, who grasped that I could not talk freely and answered all my questions without my asking. "Between the family and your crowd, we've got the whole of West Farms covered. And Saranne, we know already she's not in any of the danger spots. We've checked the drainage ditch from one end to the other. She's probably curled up someplace and gone to sleep. Melissa did that once in a trolley car and turned up safe and sound."

I knew the story. Before she'd been found, the police had dragged the pond. I couldn't ask if that was being done now, and he didn't mention it.

I hung up. The clock ticked. Five o'clock. A quarter after. Katie came in, with Mark behind her. She was full of brambles and her hair was falling down, and I looked no prize myself, but for once neither of us thought twice about it. They stopped just long enough to gulp some milk and report, and were gone again.

Aunt Tish looked in the ice box, found some chickens, and started cutting them up for frying. "Mama will have a fit if dinner isn't started."

"You don't have to do that."

*"I have to keep my hands busy."*

I didn't try to stop her.

A quarter to six. It was purple-dark now. Much worse for searching. Aunt Tish didn't want help; she didn't want company; I went into the parlor and I paced up and down. To the side window, to the door, to the fireplace. My legs wouldn't stay still, and neither would my mind.

The doorbell rang. "I'll get it!" I called sharply and ran for it, suddenly afraid. I threw the door open, and there stood Paul Hodge.

For an instant, I was so startled to see him I didn't notice the small, pale figure by his side. Then I heard Aunt Tish, in an unfamiliar voice, whisper, *"Nichola,"* and swoop down on her.

I stared at Paul with eyes that suddenly were brimming. "How did you—"

"I was over in the park by the zoo. Sitting," Paul said. His eyes flickered defensively. "Then I heard this little soft voice trying to get the guard's attention. I guess she thought he was a policeman. She kept asking for 'directions to the key, please,' and he didn't know what on earth she was talking about."

"She meant the quay," Aunt Tish said, squeezing Nichola tight. "The dock. She *was* trying to get Home."

Over Aunt Tish's shoulder, Nichola's eyes stared with their unwavering, far-seeing gaze.

"That's the way she's been, ever since we got to this street," Paul said, watching her. "Is she all right?"

I couldn't answer, not in front of Nichola and Aunt Tish. "Paul, how did you know?"

Paul's face looked as though he'd expected something better of me. "I heard her voice. She talked like a regular Limey, like what Schuyler the Great was trying to get away with at rehearsal. So I figured she must be who she is. She wouldn't tell me her name, just informed me she wasn't allowed to talk to strangers. So I said all right, I couldn't tell her how to find the key, but I could take her home, and she trotted right along. Till we got to this corner, and she saw where she was. For a minute I thought she was going to have a conniption, then suddenly she just—went like that."

We all contemplated Nichola, who was standing as tranquil and unresponsive as one of her own dolls.

Aunt Tish let her breath out heavily.

"I'd better get her to bed before the family descends." She straightened, and for the first time really looked at Paul. Something changed in her eyes.

"You're Paul Hodge, aren't you? I'm Letitia Maitland-Mayne, I was a friend of your sister Mary. Don't go, please, until I come back down."

So Paul followed me out to the kitchen and after a few moments began to help me fry chicken, snatching the pieces from the hot fat at just the right moment and depositing them neatly on the rack to dry.

"I cook for myself a lot," he murmured, noticing my astonishment. "When I come in at odd hours and stuff. You know."

My uncles clattered in and heard the good news. The air became filled with masculine camaraderie, and I could feel Paul, after his first tension, relax. Aunt Tish came back down, looking shaky but more tranquil, wanting to know the whole story. Pretty soon the rest of the family began arriving, and there was a higher noise level, more explanations.

Mark was with Katie, and they were both flabbergasted to find Paul there. Katie, hearing that Paul was hero of the hour, had the grace to look embarrassed. Mark got that sardonic expression, which meant he was annoyed.

"Well, well, nice to know you can do something right, eh, Hodge?"

The air crackled.

"If you ask me, it's a darn good thing we stopped rehearsal early today," I said loudly. And then everybody started to talk at once. I found myself looking straight across the room at Aunt Tish, and she had that odd look in her eyes again—as if she was coming up out of the mists into some knowledge that disturbed her.

Paul was performing a vanishing act, edging toward the door.

"Oh, no," Aunt Tish said in her clear, soft, faintly-accented voice. "Oh no, please, you've done so much, you'll stay and have potluck with us, won't you?"

"Course the boy'll stay," Gramp drawled. "Long past dinner hour at his house now, just hope his folks won't be mad."

"I'll call 'em," Gram said, heading for the phone, and in a moment we could hear her singing Paul Hodge's praises for what was undoubtedly the first time in her life.

The noise in the kitchen was beginning to ring in my ears, and my legs felt weak. I wandered into the dining room and sat down on a chair there, and Paul followed.

"Saranne, it's none of my business, but—is the kid all right?"

Our family has a rigid code about not washing family linen in public, especially when one doesn't know the nature of the stains, but I was too giddy to care. "She wants her father, and she wants her home. Her real home, England. And I guess they're both gone for good," I said baldly.

"Oh," Paul's monosyllable was comprehensive, so much so that I found myself going on haltingly. "She's trying to run away . . . not the way boys can, but inside herself. She, and her mother too, and we're at our wits' end, all of us."

"Isn't it natural, after what's happened to them?" Paul asked quietly.

"But it gets worse, not better. We thought once

they were here, safe . . . but I guess West Farms isn't home to Aunt Tish any more, either. They're . . . grieving the loss of London, as well as Uncle Anthony. They're as much aliens here as—as Jessica and Shylock were in Venice."

"And I guess people and things are always interwoven, a part of each other. Like when you cut a tap root on a tree, and the tree can die."

This was an absolutely astonishing conversation to be having with Paul Hodge. And yet I was, almost as if I was starved for it, responding. "That's why I feel so awful that I can't reach Nichola, or Aunt Tish, either. Because I *do* know what it's like to struggle to survive. And because I always thought—if Aunt Tish were here— she'd see that in me."

"I should think you'd have enough people around in your big family who do know you."

"Sometimes I feel swamped by all the people who think they know me and know what's best for me!"

I didn't know why that came out with so much vehemence. All I knew was that when I looked, startled, into Paul's eyes, I had the dizzying sensation of, for the first time in my life, being completely understood.

# April

# VI

I FELT CLOSE TO AUNT TISH AFTER THAT DAY; I FELT CLOSE
to Paul. Yet I still didn't know any more about them,
and on the outside nothing at all changed. I still felt
self-conscious and overprotective of Paul at rehearsals,
because by now everybody knew it was "my fault" he
was in the play—and he wasn't doing well. He came
when he wasn't needed, not when he was. He forgot,
then lost, his script. He acted flippant about the play
and insolent towards everyone. And I kept feeling I
was in some way failing them all.

At home, the only thing different was that I no
longer felt a stranger to Aunt Tish, and I knew she
hadn't lost the capacity to feel. But she was still remote,
and Nichola was still locked inside her fog.

Nichola's trying to run away had scared everybody,
so when Gramp called a Family Conference we all felt
relieved. We gathered in Gram's dining room, late Palm

Sunday afternoon, while Aunt Tish fixed nursery tea for Nichola to have upstairs. Uncle Ben frowned about that.

"Shouldn't the Punkin be here? It's her needs and her future we're talking about."

Aunt Tish shook her head. "She gets panicky when we're all together. So much noise, so many people, everything so different." She carried the tray upstairs; came down again. "Nikki's falling asleep already. She sleeps so much, Mama. She just can't get enough. She won't even listen on the stairs, the way Marnie and I used to do, remember? She's not like us." Aunt Tish shivered slightly.

"Give her time," Aunt Marnie said warmly.

"I don't know if that will help. And we may not have time. Look at the other day. God knows what could have happened if Paul hadn't—"

"Mustn't let yourself think like that," Gram said staunchly. "Look at the things you young ones survived. Led charmed lives."

"But Nichola's different," Aunt Tish said, hard. "That's what I keep seeing. I never realized it before so clearly. You have no idea how strange everything is for her here. She's lost everything familiar, not just Anthony, but Grandmama Vivienne and Nannie, and her puppy, and the house and her nursery furniture and her garden. Even the trams move on the wrong side of the street! All I had time to think of was getting where we'd be safe from the bombing raids. And where everything wouldn't hurt so much, remembering. . . . I thought it would *help*. But it's just—more loss."

There was a silence.

"It seems to me," Dad said, matter-of-fact, "that what helps children best in crisis is routine. Like what you're doing, Tish, her regular nursery tea. And get some household oddments for her like the ones she's used to."

"But can I?" Aunt Tish asked starkly. "We don't even—" She stopped; started over. "We don't even know yet if it's going to be possible for me to get money out of England. Anthony's estate—much of it's entailed, of course—but the income . . . it's supposed to be cabled to me, but who knows, with the War. . . ."

I saw Dad and Uncle Ben exchange glances.

"There's your book money," Gram said. Aunt Tish shook her head.

"I haven't been writing, since the War. I did volunteer nursing at the army hospital at Lancashire Gate . . . the same books don't keep selling well forever, you know." She ran a hand abstractedly through her hair. "I should get in touch with the publishers here, find out if there're any royalties they weren't able to send overseas . . . Oh, there's just so much. . . ."

"Seems to me if you need somebody to talk to publishers for you," Gram said clearly, "best person you could possibly get would be Kenneth Latham."

There was another silence. All at once, Aunt Tish was wary. Dad and Uncle Ben both spoke at once.

"I'm sure within the family we'll be glad to see

that you have adequate funds. As a loan," Dad added quickly, seeing the proud lift of Aunt Tish's head. "Until you get your own affairs in order."

"It seems to *me*," Ben said, "the first thing Tish and Nichola need is a home of their own. One run the way *they're* used to. Mama, with all due respect, living in your house is *not* restful." There were understanding chuckles as Gram bridled. "I don't know why I didn't think of it before. I'm baching it in the house Aunt Kate left me. Tish, if you want to move in and keep house for me, you can consider the place as yours. Run it your own way, redecorate to suit yourself."

Relief was naked on Aunt Tish's face. "It would be a godsend. Mama I don't want to sound ungrateful, but—"

"No need to apologize," Gramp said gruffly. "You're used to being head of your own household, and there isn't a woman born who could share a kitchen with your ma without a fight. Remember the share-the-work campaign before Katie was born?"

The grownups snickered. All of a sudden there was a warmth in the room that had not been there before. I could feel the tension easing from Aunt Tish. "Ben, I accept your offer. Thanks. These's no need to redecorate."

"There is for me," Uncle Ben said bluntly. "I'm still living with Aunt K's bad taste and aspidistra. I'm sick of it, just haven't had the time or known where to start. Besides, I thought we agreed it would be better for Punkin to have surroundings that look a bit familiar.

So you see to it, Sis, and I'll pay the bills. I can afford it."

Gram rose. "I'll get the coffee, since nobody can stand being in a kitchen with me." Mother and my aunts started getting cups and cake plates from the china closet.

WE WERE ALL RATHER THOUGHTFUL WALKING HOME THAT evening. "I could have kicked Mama for that remark about Ken Latham," Mother said. "Very good idea, very bad timing."

"What *is* this about Mr. Latham and Aunt Tish?"

"I don't know," Mother responded frankly. "Ther was an understanding, or I always thought so. Then Tish went to England with Marguerite Finchler Owens and did not come back. That's all anybody's ever known. Both of them can be about as eloquent as oysters about their personal affairs."

"And Latham's never married," Dad said innocently.

"And Tish bolts like a startled fawn every time his name's mentioned. It's the only time she *has* reacted, except when Nichola was lost. Oh, I'm so glad Ben had that idea about the house. And the redecorating. That should pull her out of the slough a little, don't you think?"

"At least it may keep her mind off the War," Dad said heavily.

ON MONDAY, APRIL THE SECOND, NEWSPAPER HEADLINES shrieked that President Wilson had asked Congress to declare war on the Kaiser. On April sixth, Congress passed the resolution. It was Good Friday.

The church for Good Friday service was draped in purple, crowded and silent. Mr. Derbyshire lit a red lantern hanging in one of the side shrines. It would burn, he said, as an eternal flame until the conflict ceased.

In the narthex after, blinking in the dim light, everyone was still quiet. I saw Paul Hodge, who nodded, and started his usual slipping away, but Aunt Tish had seen him. She went to him, hands outstretched.

"I want to thank you again, more than you can ever know. If there's ever anything that I can do for you. . . ."

Paul looked more embarrassed than when he was caught doing something wrong.

THE WHEELS WERE GOING AROUND IN MOTHER'S HEAD ON Saturday morning. "Obviously the only thing that can still stir Tish is Nichola. I wonder. . . ." She cranked the phone firmly. "Mama? Yes, I know it's only eight o'clock, since when did you sleep late? Is Tish up yet? . . . Tish, it just dawned on me, have you done anything about Nichola's Easter clothes? Yes, I know, but we agreed with Ben's saying usual routine would be best, and you did tell me Anthony didn't believe in wearing mourning. . . ."

Within an hour, Aunt Tish and Nichola were meeting us at the trolley. We went to Wanamakers, where Nichola acquired a pale blue broadcloth coat and a matching blue silk frock and bonnet. We had lunch at a restaurant and were serenaded by strolling violinists.

And then Mother talked Aunt Tish into going through the home furnishings department. "At least look at what's being shown," she urged. "You can't rear a child in Aunt Kate's atmosphere!"

It was so queer, it was almost as if we were speaking dialogue in a play. We would be talking perfectly naturally of trivia, laughing even, and then suddenly Aunt Tish would stop, and she would either start to shake or seem to go very far away where we could not follow. As for Nichola, she was like a doll, a perfect and well-behaved doll that could not even be wound up.

"And now," Mother said brightly, when our shopping was completed, "do you know what your mummy and I always did when our mother brought us shopping? We stopped for ice cream sodas!"

Nichola didn't even glance at her. "We always have tea and seedy cake," she said. "At Home."

Mother looked at Aunt Tish, who shrugged. She looked very tired. All at once I felt a tremendous wave of compassion for Nichola, who was trying so valiantly to swim up a strange stream. "Then I guess we'd better go home," I said gently, and Nichola let me take her hand and sit by her on the trolley. Not as if she wanted me to. As if she simply didn't care.

"YOU'RE RIGHT, BEN," AUNT TISH SAID AT EASTER DINNER. "I had better recreate the atmosphere. Perhaps a clean break is not the kindest for a child. But I don't want to move in until the changes in the house are already made."

Change was in the wind that Easter Sunday. No

one spoke of the War, yet it was omnipresent. At church, here and there, there were flurries of excitement over young men, National Guard members, already in their uniforms. Dad took the auto to the station to meet the Stamford relatives, and when they walked into the house, Gram and Aunt Annie hugged hard without speaking.

Leslie put a small diamond on Melissa's finger. "I'm going to the recruiting office first thing tomorrow. I'm applying for officers' training; there's a three-month program for fellows who have graduated college. Missy, I want us to be married *soon*."

Easter dinner was at our house. Everyone strove to be gay and cheerful, and sometimes it worked. Later the school crowd came. There was no Young Peoples' that evening, and everyone seemed to need a place to be together. Even MSS III. Even Paul.

We talked about the War; we talked about the play.

"It won't last long," Mark said confidently, referring to the former. "Once the American troops go over there, we'll wipe things up quickly."

"You as sure of that, Schuyler, as you were that we wouldn't get into it at all?" Paul asked quietly.

Nichola, to my astonishment, was snuggled up to Paul's left side. "My papa's going to drive the Kaiser back. My papa and his aeroplane. He doesn't need your help." She was speaking in the present tense, her soft voice defiant.

Everyone looked uncomfortable, except Paul who whispered, "You tell 'em, kid."

"You know what?" Katie said abruptly. "*I* think

we ought to make the play into a war relief benefit. Pa says there's bound to be some kind of civilian fund drives organized. I think we ought to make this something the whole school can rally round."

Here was something we could *do;* something to get excited about. "We'll have to clear it with administration," Mark said. His face lighted. "I'll call Mr. Moore personally tomorrow. And we can tell Miss Olsen at rehearsal. It's fortunate we're having rehearsals during spring vacation."

"In more ways than one," Tim murmured. Mark ignored the comment.

"What we need is a really solid publicity campaign. Handbills, newspaper stories, posters everywhere. We could paint a banner on a sheet and hang it across the road in front of school."

I couldn't help myself. "Don't you think you'd better be sure first the play will go well?"

Mark didn't like that. "You're not an actress, Sarah Anne. You don't understand. It will be all right on the night."

But I had none of that confidence; I couldn't. And looking across the room, I saw my own doubts reflected in Paul's eyes.

WE STARTED REHEARSING AT ONE O'CLOCK MONDAY AFTERnoon. Or, rather, we were supposed to—everyone had vacationitis and was acting silly, and I had to make four telephone calls before we could locate all the missing souls. One of them was Mark, who was not at home, and when he walked in nearly an hour late he was annoyed at the reception he received.

"I was over at Mr. Moore's, Miss Olsen, discussing making the play a school-sponsored War charity. Didn't Sarah Anne tell you?" He was angry with *me,* and Miss Olsen was so angry at him that she could scarcely speak. All she said was, "You ought not to have been doing so during rehearsal time. Get on stage, Mark, we'll discuss it later." She looked as if she didn't trust herself to say anything more.

It was absolutely the worst rehearsal yet. Kids didn't know their lines and didn't care; they clowned outrageously. Katie, who knew her lines cold, did care, and let them know it, furiously. Mark, who up to now had had the lines if not the character, started losing them. The more he did, the angrier he grew.

"Really, Saranne, if you're supposed to be prompting, *prompt.* Don't leave me groping. Otherwise don't set yourself up as Little Aid to Teacher."

I could have thrown the script at him. Next time, when I did come in quickly, he snapped that I was interrupting his dramatic pause.

Paul was another of the latecomers, and he too did not know his lines. The bitterness, the restlessness were there, but it was Paul's bitterness, not that of an elderly Italian Jewish man. And having him and Mark in dialogue together was disastrous. Mark was baiting Paul, as Bassanio would not dare bait Shylock. Miss Olsen kept them going over and over the same pages, and always the same things were wrong.

"No. Do it again. Saranne, read Shylock's line for him."

"All right! I heard it!"

"But, Paul, you're twisting two speeches together, and it changes the whole thing. Listen—"

"I said I know!" Paul swung round at me, his eyes burning. "You're not personally responsible for me, or Shylock, so stop trying to mother hen me through it, will you?"

"Could we just get on with the scene?" Katie asked coldly.

I sat down again, my eyes stinging, and after a moment Tim's voice picked up with Gratiano's lines, and the scene went on. Ran into the same dead end. For a second the air sizzled. Then Paul flung his script down.

"Oh, what the hell's the use?"

He said it under his breath, but Mark heard, and returned, pointedly. "One may well ask."

"That is enough." Miss Olsen's voice was low, so low it was a moment before everyone realized she was shaking with rage. "There will be no rehearsals at all if your hearts aren't in it. Come back at one o'clock tomorrow, and *on time*. And before you go ahead with your grandiose plans, you had better make up your minds whether you are willing to invest the effort to make a play worth seeing."

She gathered her papers together and left.

Tim Molloy whistled comprehensively.

"Saranne," Katie was saying, "walk home with me,

will you? Tish wanted you to stop for tea with her and Nichola."

I wanted to talk to Miss Olsen. I needed to talk to Miss Olsen, but the family needed me. So I went with Katie, uneasily conscious that Miss Olsen looked very much alone.

We didn't talk much going home. Aunt Tish had a tea table set up in the parlor, and Gram's silver service polished. She'd made Nichola's seedy cake and little almond tarts called Maids of Honor. "They're one of the first things I learned to make in England. How did the play rehearsal go?"

Aunt Tish was making an effort, and we tried to help her, but Nichola perched like a prim little old lady on her footstool and was silent. Katie described rehearsals wittily, trying to make Nichola laugh, but soon her own pent-up feelings came exploding out. "It's just awful, Tish! We're making absolute fools of ourselves, and there's no way out, because nobody knows what to do to make it better."

"They could try a little harder," I said flatly.

Katie looked at me. "It's easy for you to say. You're not in it. And your coming down on everybody like a Dutch uncle doesn't help things, either. All you're doing is making people hate you."

"Katie, that's not fair! It's *my* job, and they're just fooling around as if they don't care—"

"They care. Why do you think they act that way? They're just covering up because we're all floundering. Mark's sounding like his father in a political campaign, and Lord knows what Paul's apt to sound like from one rehearsal to another, and I wish I could just walk out except then *I'd* be the one to get all the blame." Katie turned to Tish, her voice choking. "Couldn't you come to rehearsal, and at least tell me what I'm doing right or wrong? Because so help me God, I won't get up on that stage if I have to be ashamed."

Aunt Tish looked startled and, oddly, panicked. "Oh, I—couldn't."

"Yes, you could," Katie said doggedly. "You're Browning Society, and you're famous, and everybody knows what a good actress you've been. You're the only person I know who could help me, if you could spare the time from being the Tragic Queen."

"*Katherine!*" Gram said.

"I mean it, Mama. We had all those big speeches about how Tish has been through so much and how she needs us, and about how having things to do helps people work through grief. Well, Tish is my sister, and I need *her,* if she cares enough."

"All right, Katie. You made your point." It was Aunt Tish who spoke. "I'll come tomorrow, if you call your teacher first and ask if it's all right."

Katie was on the way to the phone when it began to shrill. "Yes, she is. Who's calling?" we heard her say, and then, "No, Mrs. Maitland-Mayne is not giving out interviews."

The newspaper vultures were descending again. Now they wanted personal stories on how Letitia Chambers Sterling felt about America entering the War. Or how it felt being a War widow returning to the old home country. Or would Letitia Chambers Sterling care to write her memoirs? Or a feature on Life as a Wife and Mother in War-torn London?

Finally, we left the phone off the hook. And it was I who went to Miss Olsen, before the start of next rehearsal, to feel her out on Katie's request.

"Anything your aunt would care to do would be a godsend," Miss Olsen said. She looked as though she had been crying. "I never should have started this. Directing Shakespeare demands more than I'm equipped to give it, especially right now, and that's the truth."

"Miss Olsen, please! Don't feel so bad. And don't take Katie's asking Aunt Tish as a slur on you. If the kids would only work more—"

Miss Olsen shook her head and smiled tiredly. "You're a nice girl, Saranne. But Katie's right, and you know it. I *am* over my head." She took a deep breath. "We'll muddle through, somehow. And Saranne, don't you go thinking the burden's on *your* shoulders."

TUESDAY'S REHEARSAL WAS MUCH LIKE MONDAY'S, BUT without explosions. Wednesday's was different, because Aunt Tish was there. She sat quietly, making notes, and at first everyone was terribly self-conscious. Slowly, though, things improved. It was not Portia's Venice, but it was certainly a lot better than it had been.

When it was over, everyone turned toward Aunt Tish expectantly, but she seemed not to see. She went to Miss Olsen and spoke with her for a few minutes, softly, so no one could hear. Then left.

"Come home with me," Katie begged me, watching her go.

"I thought you'd had enough of my being Little Mouthpiece for Director."

"Don't rub it in. I wanted Tish here, but now I'm scared." That was something for Katie to admit.

I went home with her, and Tish, over the teacups, was brutally blunt. "It's embarrassing to watch, which is a shame, because it could be so good. The cast has exactly the right qualities for the roles, if they had the discipline, or the courage, as the case may be. As for you, Kate, you're selling out and showing off."

Katie flushed. "I don't want to spill my insides out if no one else is going to."

Tish just looked at her. "Why not, if the play needs it? Or are you afraid of what you might discover? I couldn't tell whether you wanted us to think you were being real, when you weren't, or to not know it when you were. Art is exposure, Katie. Either make up your mind to that, or give it up." Katie couldn't answer. Quietly, Tish laid the notebook by her hand. "You asked for these. If you want me to go over and explain them later, I will."

It wasn't till she'd gone off with Nichola, and Katie had had more tea to restore her equilibrium, that we appreciated what Aunt Tish had done. There were twelve pages of tightly written script, pinpointing exactly what was wrong and how to fix it.

Katie shook her head. "Why couldn't we have had direction like this from the beginning?"

"Do you really think it would have made any difference? Or will now?"

Katie's shoulders sagged. "*I* don't know. I *do* want to try. But even if I do knock down the walls . . . it still won't make the whole play come together. Or make the others real."

"It may *have* to come from you. Because Paul's still an unknown quantity the kids won't listen to, and . . ." I stopped, tactfully, but Katie took a deep breath and her defenses crumbled.

"Go ahead, say it. It's Mark's responsibility as president to build morale and make us care, and he won't. Or can't."

For a minute, everything was very still.

"I thought he was so wonderful," Katie said raggedly. "I thought he could do anything. Like what Mama's always telling us to look for when we're shopping; 'First quality, no flaws.' And ever since this horrible play started I keep seeing flaws pop out like chicken pox, more each day. Only I still think he's wonderful. That's crazy, isn't it?"

I was certainly in no position to answer that.

I felt even more disoriented when I received a telephone call from Paul that afternoon.

"Saranne, I just wondered—did your aunt say anything that could help with Shylock?"

In the midst of my astonishment, my ears still registered his choice of words. Not was he good, or how did he do, but what could be improved. I marshalled my thoughts to give him as accurate a report of Aunt Tish's criticism as I could remember, hoping that maybe Katie and I wouldn't have the whole burden of salvage operations on our shoulders, after all.

Mark didn't ask either Katie or me for such critique.

My disoriented feeling intensified at rehearsal Friday afternoon. There was a different kind of current in the air. Miss Olsen was preoccupied, abstracted, and made few interruptions. Had she just given up, I wondered, or what? About half an hour into rehearsal the door opened softly and Aunt Tish slipped inside. I hadn't expected her; I don't think Katie even saw her as she took a chair quietly at the back.

We got into the trial scene. Paul pulled that knife out of his boot. Katie made a swift, involuntary gesture of recoil. It was right for Portia, but it wasn't Portia because she was not yet onstage. *Katie was afraid.* That was it, wasn't it? The picture clicked suddenly into sharp focus, overlaid on all those old stories of Paul back through the years. The fire everyone believed that he had set. The fires he *had* set when he was a child. That awful story Aunt Kate had believed, of how he'd hanged a kitten, instead of been trying to rescue it the way he'd claimed.

That was why the snickering about the knife when Paul had stropped it. Not just Katie, but the others, even Mark, were truly and genuinely afraid of what Paul might do. And so the laughter, the put-downs, the holding-off—Paul was not only different, he was dangerous. If I did not see him so, it was because I was naive—

or because I'd seen a gentler side of Paul that none of the others had.

There was no snickering about the knife today. But again, Mark as Bassanio was baiting Paul, making the written lines sharp with a personal threat. Mark was coming back with a calculated retort for everything Paul said or did. Private, demeaning resentment as I'd thought? Or was Mark, feeling his responsibility as president, trying to exercise authority over a potentially dangerous situation, just as Miss Olsen was trying futilely to assert authority over the play?

Paul was frightening even me with the distillation of hatred he was pouring out in the scene. When he spoke, the yellow schoolroom walls, the varnished desks melted away. I felt my skin crawl, and the air was thick. He forgot a line; made it up in modern slang. Forgot again and cursed beneath his breath. I saw Mark drop out of character and go to him, speaking firmly. I couldn't hear his words, but we all heard Paul's.

"What the hell's the use! You want a scapegoat to kick around? Look somewhere else! I'm fed to the teeth with pearls being thrown to swine!"

Paul flung the knife from his hand and it hit the floor, clattering. Paul's arm sent the door flying open. Then he was gone, pounding down the hall, vanishing across the lawn.

My mind was still too taken aback at Paul Hodge quoting the Bible to wonder who he meant was casting pearls, and who was swine. I didn't recognize at first another, shocking sound.

Miss Olsen, pushing back her chair so hard it screeched. She didn't say a word; she couldn't; she was shaking, and her knuckles were pressed against her mouth. She just stood there a moment, as all of us were caught in silence, and then she walked out. Aunt Tish followed.

There was a sticky pause. Katie looked at me, and I acted by instinct. "Rehearsal's over. Go home and study your scripts. I'll see that you get notes."

My voice had a calm, unusual authority, and it was respected. Tim and two others quietly began putting the room back in order. As quietly, the others murmured good-bye and left. Finally I was alone. Miss Olsen did not return. Aunt Tish did not return. I gathered my things together and went out, closing the door behind me. Around the corner of the echoing corridor, two figures were sitting on a window ledge. Over Miss Olsen's bent head, Aunt Tish's eyes signaled me to leave them there, and I did.

Katie was waiting for me out on the lawn, and we walked home together, but we didn't talk much.

On Saturday, April 14, President Wilson created the Committee of Public Information. In church that Sunday there were more uniforms. When we reached school Monday morning, Miss Olsen wasn't there. A substitute was teaching Miss Olsen's class. Rehearsal for that afternoon was cancelled. At lunch, Abby said she had heard Miss Olsen wasn't coming back at all.

"What about the play?"

Abby's eyes widened. "Who knows? Maybe it was

too much for her! My mother heard she went all to pieces at rehearsal Friday."

"Your mother's an idiot," Katie snapped. She pushed her chair back and went flying off in the direction of MSS III, and I followed.

Lagging discreetly, I couldn't hear her words clearly, or see her face, but I did see Mark's shrug; I caught the tone of his "Perhaps it's just as well."

Katie's head came back as if she'd been slapped. "You hypocrite," she said, softly and distinctly. "You make such a big thing about being president, and you really don't give a damn."

I got out of there before Katie turned and saw me; got out, literally. I walked straight out of the lunchroom and ran down the hall to Mr. Moore's office.

Mr. Moore looked up, his smile fading. "What is it, Saranne? I can see something's wrong."

"Is it true Miss Olsen's left and isn't coming back?"

He hesitated; nodded. "There will be a public announcement tomorrow. She's asked to be released from her contract. Her fiancé is entering the service, and he wants her to go back to Wisconsin and be married before he goes overseas. I believe she's been under a great deal of stress, because she didn't believe it was right for her to walk away from her responsibilities here. Apparently over the weekend something happened to change her mind."

"Mr. Moore . . . what about the play?"

"I'm afraid that will have to be given up. It's highly unlikely we can find a teacher to take over on such short notice."

I thought of the look on Katie's face just now. I thought of what Paul had said, and Paul's calling me for Aunt Tish's criticism, and a whole lot more. And I said, "Mr. Moore, could you excuse me from school for the rest of the day? I can't explain, but I may know a way we can still have the play, and it is important."

Somewhat to my astonishment, he did not press me. He looked at me and said, "You're a nice girl, Saranne," in a tone that was a big improvement on the way I usually heard that phrase, and wrote me out a pass.

I had to get out early because I didn't want to talk to Aunt Tish in front of Gram or Katie. I knew all the reasons why it was wrong for me to ask this of her. I also knew that I couldn't live with myself if I didn't ask it.

At least Aunt Tish didn't interrupt or refuse at once, although I saw that wary, pressured look I feared as soon as I had blurted out my request. "I know it isn't fair to ask you," I wound up. "You just got here, you're busy fixing up the house, and—everything. But Katie was right, you're the only one who could pick up the pieces. And it's terribly important that the play go on."

"Important for Katie, or for you?" Aunt Tish asked quietly.

"I don't know," I answered honestly. "For the War effort, first of all. Then to show that Browning Society hasn't gone to the snobs. But mostly for Paul Hodge. This is the first thing he's ever done that he could be proud of, and it's just not right to have it yanked out from under him."

Aunt Tish got that strange look everyone always

got when Paul Hodge was mentioned. I flushed. "I suppose you think I'm crazy, too, getting worked up about the Salvation of St. Paul, as Katie calls it."

"Hardly," Aunt Tish said inscrutably. She stared off into space, and then she straightened. "I had a feeling you'd ask me this. Because, as you've guessed, I did have a part in Miss Olsen's leaving. All right, Saranne, I'll do it. *If* Browning Society, especially the cast, wants me to, and if they agree to do things exactly as I say."

The next afternoon there was a hastily called meeting of the entire Society. Aunt Tish was blunt. "If you seriously want to work—with me, with one another— then I'll help you. Not otherwise."

Mark cleared his throat. "I don't think there's any question in anybody's mind," he said quietly, and my opinion of him went up some notches. Paul said nothing, but he was *there*—I'd spent fifteen minutes finding him, and another twenty persuading him to come, but no one need know that. Katie was simply flabbergasted that I'd had the nerve to approach Aunt Tish.

"So Tish's social conscience is still operating. Smart thinking," Gram said to me in private. "Least it's getting her back out in the world. Now if we could just figure out how to light a fire under the young one!"

All of us were making special efforts where Nichola was concerned, but nothing seemed of any use. She was like Sleeping Beauty imprisoned in a spell.

Rehearsals resumed, and rehearsals with Aunt Tish were different. They began on time, they ended promptly, and if they weren't fun, they weren't torture either. More, the real bones of the play began to show. Katie's Portia grew more womanly, and little by little, Mark's Bassanio grew more human. Afterwards we walked home together, Aunt Tish and Katie and I—sometimes Nichola, for Aunt Tish had arranged that she could be brought to watch rehearsals after her own lessons were through. No one knew what Nichola thought of the proceedings, but she smiled when Paul was there. Everyone knew what Aunt Tish thought was good or not good, and why. What they didn't know was whether she thought the play would improve enough in time.

*I* knew, because it was with me that Aunt Tish shared her own worries, questions, doubts about the play. "I'm so glad you're working with me," Aunt Tish said. "You know the people, you understand them, and I'm a stranger."

"Sometimes I think I don't understand at all."

"Oh yes, you do," Aunt Tish smiled. "You under-estimate yourself, Saranne. You're much more of a heal-ing force here than you realize."

I treasured these private conferences because Aunt Tish treated me not just as a confidante but as an equal. She consulted me on how to handle people, and I strove to live up to what she saw in me. But this separated me even further from the others.

"I feel like a pariah," I said to Katie, and she shrugged and said, "Well, what can you expect?"

But how could I tell Katie that Tish was afraid her Aunt Kate pride and stubbornness might not let her show vulnerability onstage any more than off, that she wondered if Paul could ever trust anyone enough to take a chance, that she sensed Mark was really respecting her direction, but something in him wouldn't let him follow it in public?

"Why don't you rip the skin off him in private?" I suggested.

Tish gave me a startled look. "You have a point. I wish you'd suggested that to me this afternoon."

"I can't make suggestions at rehearsals."

"Yes, you can. You know I've asked you to. You needn't worry I'll use them if they're not good ones."

"It isn't that. It's because the kids . . . Oh, Tish—" I stopped. "I'm sorry. When we talk like this I forget to treat you as an aunt, and the crowd never forgets that I *am* your niece, and it feels like I'm taking advantage of that to act important."

She nodded as if she understood. At least she didn't press me to make comments where everyone would see me do it.

After that day, following my suggestion, she began having each of the cast in turn over to the house for tea and a serious discussion of their roles.

Mother laughed ruefully over that. "Deep down, Tish hasn't changed. She still doesn't do anything by halves."

Everyone in the family was giving me credit for getting Aunt Tish involved, even though I myself didn't understand how I'd done it. I felt guilty, and they felt relieved that between rehearsals and the coaching sessions and the shopping for the little house, she didn't have a minute for herself.

Meanwhile, America had embarked on an orgy of patriotism; reminders of the war were everywhere. Flags and recruiting posters flowered on every corner. People were singing "Over There!," "Tipperary," "Keep the Home Fires Burning." Aunt Tish flinched at that one, and when at rehearsal Mark began talking about enlisting after graduation, her face grew white and Katie changed the subject quickly.

"Reporters," Katie told me grimly. "They're still pestering for interviews. And Miss Sadie, when you were all up for dinner last Sunday, didn't help."

A wave of anti-German feeling was sweeping the country. Suddenly, German potato salad was Liberty salad, people avoided sauerkraut, and a movement was on to ban German books and language and music from the schools. Aunt Sadie was on the bandwagon for this.

"Aunt Sadie's dug up a story about how the Hodges changed their name from Hartz," I explained one afternoon. "I have to help Paul learn his lines this afternoon, and I don't dare have him come to the house. We're doing it at yours, instead."

Katie looked at me. "That, my dear, is more than *German* prejudice. And not very smart of you, if you want my opinion, which you don't. Well, if Paul's coming over, I'll make myself scarce."

Katie took herself to the library to study, and I waited, wondering as the clock ticked on, if Paul had forgotten. He hadn't had to be at rehearsal that afternoon. The tea I'd made was getting cold, and the Maids of Honor I'd baked, as Aunt Tish had shown me, went uneaten. All at once with painful clarity I saw another picture. Paul and me, around the tea table in the parlor. Me pouring tea as Aunt Tish did, graciously; serving the little almond tarts, dispensing encouragement, sympathy over forgotten lines, advice. Dispensing in a borrowed house an atmosphere of warmth and serenity. The great lady being kind to the peasant, as Katie had once suggested? Or something even more embarrassing?

The doorbell rang. I smoothed my hair back from my scarlet face.

Paul was out of breath and rumpled. "Sorry I'm late—hope you didn't think that I forgot—"

"It's all right. You didn't have to run."

"That wasn't why. Look, do you think Nichola would like to have this? Some guys were throwing stones at it, I couldn't find an owner, and I didn't know where else to take it." He hauled out a small brown puppy with stubby legs and terrified eyes.

"Throwing *stones!*"

"Because dachsunds are *Germans*," Paul said with heavy sarcasm. "Therefore obviously this is a vicious ferocious beast." He stroked a velvet ear as the puppy cowered against his shirt. "If I take it home, my dad will drown it."

I did the only thing I could. I called Aunt Tish. She, after one shocked exclamation, called Nichola, who took the puppy straight into her arms.

"Guess they've got a lot in common," Paul murmured, looking after them as they went upstairs. I looked at him, conscious that I was seeing a side of him few saw. His shirt was torn, and his cheek and knuckles scraped. I didn't ask details; I put the kettle on to make more tea.

Paul followed me into the kitchen. The front doorbell rang, and Aunt Tish called, "I'll get it." Her feet tapped, running down the stairs. There were voices, hers and a man's, insistent. "I'm sorry. I do not give interviews. You've been told—"

"Not by you directly. Nobody can get to you, if you'll excuse my saying so. Now, I'm sorry, ma'am, but I'm not going without a story. And the *Journal*'s willing on any terms you want. Interview, first-person as-told-to, or a bylined article or series by Letitia Maitland-Mayne herself—"

"I will not write about the War." Her voice was cracking. With one accord, Paul and I moved toward the hall.

She was trapped, for the man had wedged himself in the doorway, and it was clear that if she walked away he would follow. Letitia Chambers Sterling could have handled him, but not this bone-weary woman who'd been putting up with us all afternoon. Paul loomed forward. "You heard what the lady said. She doesn't want to be bothered."

The man looked Paul up and down and made the mistake of trying to ease the situation with a laugh. "Look, sonny, I don't know what you've got to do with this, but the lady and I are talking business, so keep your nose out—"

"You've got that backwards. You're the one who's

trespassing. So just get your big fat nosiness off her doorstep." The suggestion was accompanied by a shove. All at once the reporter was sprawled on the porch, and Paul and I were out there, too. I heard Aunt Tish slam and bolt the door behind us.

The reporter came up swinging, clipping Paul on the cheekbone that was already bruised. Paul reacted from instinct. His hands grabbed the man by hip and shoulder, spun him round, sent him hurtling down the steps onto the path below. "And don't come back," Paul shouted, breathing hard.

"You young hooligan, you could have killed . . . I'll have you up on charges . . ."

For a second it all hung in the balance, then the stranger took a few lumbering steps backward to the street, and fled.

I grabbed Paul and dragged him around the porch.

"Where are we going?"

"Where he can't find us, if he comes back with help."

I led him down the side steps, through the lilac bushes and cautiously through Gram's roses to the yard of Uncle Ben's house. There was a section of lattice loose below the porch, and we wriggled under.

"Katie and I used to play house here when we were little. When Aunt Kate didn't catch us, that was. Don't sit up too fast, you'll bump your head. Paul," I added, "I don't know what we'd do without you."

"That's a switch." Paul's voice twisted. He lay on his back, his hands beneath his head. His chest was still rising and falling hard from the exertion, and he stared at the cobwebby floor above us.

"Paul, don't be like that."

"Like what?"

"You know. Expecting everyone to be against you, or to feel you owe them something."

"Don't be naive, Saranne. Ninety-eight percent of the time I'm only anticipating what's already there, and you know it."

"And what about the other two percent? What about Miss Olsen? She just wanted you to have a fair chance to be good at something."

"*And* to have me make her play look good."

"What was wrong with that? It doesn't hurt you, does it? What about my aunt? Should she feel ashamed of accepting the things you've done for her? Or do you think she's only been helping you with Shylock to pay you for them?"

"What about you?" Paul rolled over on his side and looked at me. "Aren't you being Little Miss Do-Gooder? Helping out Browning Society and that rotten Hodge guy? Helping him learn his lines so he won't disgrace himself. Helping the directors. Trying to make everything peaches and cream."

"That's not fair." Embarrassment, pain, and anger choked my voice. "*All right,* I want you to be good as Shylock, I want you to be very good, because you can, and because I think you've gotten a rotten deal and it's darn unfair. I want everybody in the play to be good, and all I get for it is a lot of snickers and sarcasm and resentment. I don't want people to be hurt. I don't want you to be hurt. It tears me up when you are, and when you hurt yourself. And if you think I'm getting any . . . personal satisfaction out of 'do-gooding,' 'aid to the director,' Mr. Paul Chip-on-the-Shoulder Hodge, you're out of whatever it is you call your mind!"

The tears were rolling down my cheeks, but I was not going to be seen wiping them away. I just lay there, blinking hard, and I heard Paul say, in a very different voice, "You're right. I was unfair. You really do hurt when other people are hurting, don't you?"

"I suppose you think that's pretty silly."

"No. Just pretty rare." He lay back on the ground, not looking at me, and the fragile feeling of communion lingered. I was very conscious of his presence close beside me, but the tension in the air was gone. After a time he said, quietly, "I hope I didn't hurt that guy. I don't always know what I do when I start swinging."

"It's a very good thing for us you *did* start swinging."

"That's not usually the majority opinion. Not even mine. It scares me, sometimes, to think what I could do when I get mad."

There was something in his voice that made me dare what I had never dreamed of saying. "Did you ever think that maybe that's why people—act as they do towards you? Not because of . . . personal dislike, or the way *you* act, but because they're afraid? Because they really don't know *you* at all, not enough to trust you, they only know all those stories about violence. The fights. The fires."

"I didn't set the house afire," Paul said quietly. He was staring up at the splintery boards above us. "I came home and found my dad's chair on fire, and him in it, passed out drunk. He'd done it before, smoking and letting his cigarette drop—Ma'd been half out of her mind, afraid something like that would happen. He'd set fire to her pet lace curtains once. She warned him that if it happened again, if he couldn't get his drinking under control, she'd clear out. I don't know what either of us would do then," Paul said starkly. "She tries. All she can. I know that, even if— Anyway, when I found the fire started, all I could think was, get it out, make it look like an accident. Only it—got away from me. And it didn't look like an accident."

"But didn't you tell what really happened?"

"I didn't want my mother to find out. Besides, who'd have believed me anyway? I'd gotten rid of the evidence."

"Surely your father—"

"I thought he might appreciate it. That was a laugh. He didn't even remember. He believed the worst, along with all the rest."

"But if you told him—"

"It wouldn't make any difference. My father hates me," Paul said simply.

That was what shook me, that there was no bitterness; that it was an old, old story past caring about.

I started to murmur, "Oh, Paul," and could not go on.

Paul was looking at me in a kind of wonder. "I

don't know what made me tell you that. I don't want anyone to know the truth about it, ever."

"I won't tell," I whispered round the lump in my throat. "I promise." And then I stopped. We stared at each other, and my heart was pounding.

I heard him whisper, "Saranne—" huskily, and then I saw his face transfigured as his mouth came down on mine.


# VII

PAUL KISSED ME. NO, I'LL BE HONEST: WE KISSED EACH other. I started to cry some more. He took me in his arms and we clung together, and then wordlessly, awkwardly, we went back to the house. Gram and Gramp were home, and dinner odors were coming from the kitchen stove.

"You'd better both stay for dinner," Aunt Tish said. She was still wraithlike, but more serene. "You still haven't had a chance to work on Shylock's lines."

Paul telephoned home; he was terse, and spoke in tones we could not hear. I telephoned, and when I got finished telling Dad about the fracas with the reporter, he had Aunt Tish get on the line and give particulars so he could call the paper as her lawyer.

"Just to forestall further attempts or charges," she said, hanging up.

Katie came home from the library, looked at Paul

and me oddly, but didn't pry. Nichola came downstairs, cuddling the puppy. "He's called Paul Anthony."

Gram darted a sharp look at Aunt Tish, whose face went still with pain. Paul saw it. "That's quite a mouthful. Why don't you call him Antonio, like the character in our play?"

Nichola shook her head. "He's Captain Paul Anthony, of the Royal Air Force. I'll make him a jacket with an insignia like Papa's on it, and then nobody will dare to call him German." She hugged him tightly.

She followed Paul around like a shadow, and Paul was very kind to her. He was good with children. "You should have had younger brothers and sisters," I said, striving to sound natural.

"I guess I was enough of a shock to my parents. Sixteen years after my sister Mary. Ma's always saying she hadn't bargained on raising a second family."

We had felt so—*right,* together, without pretenses or defenses, in the little private world beneath the porch. Here among the others, everything was different, strained.

We ate, with Gramp and Uncle Peter providing casual conversation, and Aunt Melissa bustling in at last, her head spinning. Leslie had been accepted for Officers' Training Camp, and they were making plans for a military wedding. "In June, Mama. Leslie doesn't want to wait until his training's over, because he could be shipped out right away." That sent Gram into the expected tizzy, but amid all the excitement four were silent. Me. Paul. Tish and Katie, watching us.

Paul and I went into Gramp's study to work on his

lines, but that only made things worse. Paul was forgetting what he'd known before and cussing beneath his breath, then turning red, and I could not sound natural to save my soul.

Paul saw me home in silence, acting as if he half hated me. When we reached our house I stopped at the foot of the path, well out of the pool of light coming from the door. "We didn't get much work done on your lines."

"I'm sorry I wasted your time."

"You didn't! It's my job to help, and besides, you were a lifesaver, and you know it. I don't know what Letitia would have done—" I stopped. "Honestly, I feel like a Gramophone record that's gotten stuck! Paul Hodge, how long is it going to take you to believe you're good to have around?"

"Probably never. And it's not part of your job to convince me, so don't think you have to."

"Hasn't it registered on you that I *want* to? That it's *right?*"

I meant his being in the play, his helping Aunt Tish and Nichola and me, but all of a sudden the words referred to a whole lot more. We stood, staring at each other. It was Paul who spoke, and his voice was ragged.

"A whole lot more's happening than we bargained for, isn't it?"

"Yes, it is." Another stillness. I groped for words. "I'm sorry. It was awful tonight, and I didn't help."

"Don't worry," Paul said brusquely. "I won't embarrass you. You can just go back to where it hadn't happened."

"We can't go back. And I don't want to."

"You do have guts, don't you?" Paul said huskily. He took my hands in his and bent towards me. I thought he was going to kiss my mouth again, but he just pressed his lips against my forehead gently. And went, in silence.

NO GOING BACK. THAT, AND THE WHOLE DREAMLIKE SCENE beneath the porch—was it courage, or just the recognition of the inevitable? Something was changed, and it was not just that Paul had held me in his arms. It had started much earlier. Looking back, I could see the turning points along the way. Way back to when I had first seen Paul as Shylock, had first sensed more in him than the surface showed. What was different now was that we had recognized it, and because of that others did, as well.

Not through anything we said or did. Paul was scrupulously careful not to embarrass me. When Katie and I walked to school next morning we encountered Paul loitering, but on the far side of the street, where I could easily not see him. It was I who smiled first; it was Katie who asked derisively, "Well, are you going to walk along with us or aren't you?" But in school, in the mysterious way such things happen, our names were coupled. "Where's Hodge?" Mark asked impatiently when I reached rehearsal first. And Tim ambled up to say, "Tell Paul I can run lines with him if he wants, unless that would cramp your style."

"Tell him yourself. And I don't know what that's supposed to mean," I replied, embarrassed.

"Oh, come on," Tim retorted amiably. "We know each other from playpen days, remember? Look, if you see the swan in the ugly duckling, more power to you. I'm on your side. I only hope you know what you're biting off."

Rehearsal was strangely guarded. Everyone was being very courteous to each other. Aunt Tish looked tired. Katie's voice kept slipping into that superior tone; when I pointed it out, Katie looked at me as though she hated me. Paul looked furious when Tim, meaning to be funny, made a crack about, "What kind of lines was it you were working on yesterday?" And Mark—

I frowned, feeling more and more uncomfortable as rehearsal went along. Was it my imagination, or was Mark deliberately focusing his charm in my direction? "Saranne, let's look back at the notes you have on this." "Saranne, how do you think that went?" Smiling intimately. Leaning forward, his arm carelessly along the back of my chair as our heads bent together. It made my face flame to think how I once would have fed upon these marks of his attention. Now, they just made me sick.

"Can we get on with this rehearsal or would you rather concentrate on private coaching?" Paul said with heavy sarcasm.

Mark's eyebrow rose. What's the matter, Hodge, afraid of the competition? Or is it just the *Deutsch* courage coming out?"

"I'm waiting," Aunt Tish's voice snapped tersely.

Rehearsal went on, in fits and crackling spurts. It

was over, leaving everyone with an uncompleted feeling. Aunt Tish gathered her things and went, not waiting for me. Katie, too, left. When Paul saw me waiting he fell in beside me and we moved down the hall, leaving a little eddy of whispers in our wake.

"Don't say anything. It isn't worth it," I murmured, referring both to the flurry and to Mark's earlier rudeness.

"I'm trying. You don't know how hard it is." Paul's face was grim.

"It's just Mark."

"It's not just Mark. It's a whole pack of other people, including yellow journalists like that one at your house yesterday. My dad was born in this country, his father was a Forty-Eighter, had to leave the old country because he was a freedom fighter then. And now, just because people found out somehow that our name once had a Hun spelling, his business is falling off. No wonder he's so anti the human race." Paul laughed without humor. "How dumb I've been! You know I've been trying for years to figure out why everybody expected the worst of me, ever since I was a little kid? Even my old man. I guess it wasn't personal prejudice at all. Just expectation of the worst from my lousy German blood."

"Don't talk like that," I said sternly. "Not to me. Not ever."

"I warned you that getting involved with me would mess up your life."

He was determined to have a fight, any fight, and I wouldn't play. "We've got to concentrate on your lines." That at least was safe. We went to Uncle Ben's, but we sat on the porch, not under it, and we were painfully conscious not to touch.

I WAS LATE HOME FOR DINNER. MOTHER DIDN'T COMMENT, but she kept looking at me with searching glances that were an invitation to confide. I ignored them; I went upstairs and tried unsuccessfully to concentrate on schoolwork that was falling behind.

The doorbell rang. Mother's voice called, "Saranne, Katie's here," and Katie's footsteps were on the stairs. She was in my room, shutting the door behind her.

"I have to talk to you."

I motioned toward a chair. "Why didn't you wait for me this afternoon?"

"I scarcely thought you'd notice." The bitterness in her voice took my breath away. I stared at her.

"This can't be us," I said at last, shakily. "What's going on?"

"*You* tell *me*," Katie retorted. "I feel as if I don't know you any more. Saranne Albright, what are you after?"

I was totally baffled, and then light dawned. "Are you talking about Mark this afternoon? Oh, Katie, I'm sorry, I don't know why he was acting that way, but I didn't want it."

Katie batted that away. "*I* know why, and so do you. Because he couldn't stand to have a girl who's got power and influence in the school falling over somebody else instead of him. I know you didn't want him, it showed in your face; he'd have seen it too, if he'd let himself." She gave a bitter chuckle. "It's funny, really. I used to be afraid that you were sweet on Mark, and that he'd like you better because you really are a nicer person than I am. But you aren't, are you? All the talk about defending the innocent and crusading for the waifs and strays, and you really pulled the wool over our eyes good."

"Katie Allison, I honestly don't know what you're talking about."

Katie looked squarely at me with accusing eyes. "I saw you and Paul under the porch next door yesterday."

I didn't say anything because I couldn't. I didn't look away; I could at least be proud I had the backbone not to look away. It was Katie who did. She asked at last, in a low voice, "I didn't tell. I swear to God, Saranne, I'll never tell. But are you honestly going to try to tell me there isn't anything between you and Paul Hodge?"

"I'm not going to try to tell you anything," I said with dignity. "Any more than you can tell me exactly what and why you feel for Mark." I drew a deep breath. "But if you were spying on us then you know there wasn't anything—wrong."

"Yet."

"Katie Allison, what do you think I am?"

"Hell and damn!" Katie exploded. She grabbed me by the shoulders and shook me hard. "I think you're human, Sarah Anne Albright, and you'd better stop hiding behind that dreamy innocence before you get hurt. Paul Hodge is bad news, and if you weren't so naive and stubborn you'd admit it. I know you're a sucker for the underdog, but where—"

"Don't you *dare* say where there's smoke there's fire!"

"All right, I won't. But drat it, I don't want you hurt. When a girl like you gets mixed up with somebody like him—"

"Somebody like him," I said distinctly, "just happens to be the kindest and the most courageous person I've ever known. Also the most understanding, which is something I've been pretty short of lately, especially from you."

"All right," Katie said at last. "It's no use my talking. You're right, we can't understand some things, especially things like this. But don't expect me to say I'm sorry, because I'm not."

Things were happening too fast. I felt as if I were living in disconnected pieces. The play was two and a half weeks away; none of us knew whether it would pull together in that time. What was worse, Aunt Tish looked up at rehearsal Wednesday afternoon and asked, "By the way, what is being done about sets and costumes?" and the roof fell on us with a thud. We had been so preoccupied with rehearsals that no one had thought about it. "I had not realized I had responsibility for production also," Aunt Tish said in a very neutral voice. "Mark, we had better have a conference immediately after rehearsal."

Mark cleared his throat. "Don't worry, we'll have things rolling within twenty-four hours," he said with his usual briskness, but he looked shocked at the discovery of how he'd let things slide.

Parents could be drawn in for help with carpentry or sewing, but there was no money for necessary supplies. We planned, hastily, a dance in the gym that Saturday night. "Make it for War Relief," Mr. Moore suggested. "You'll get more support, and that's what you're doing the play for, anyway. Then you can borrow from the dance proceeds for expense money against your ticket sales."

It was true, what people said about crises galvanizing energy and welding bonds. All at once, the play mattered; all at once, people worked together. No time for decorating? We borrowed flags, stood them down the length of the gym, hung walls with bunting. Aunt Tish went down to the secretarial school, borrowed a typewriter, batted out publicity releases for dance and play. Everybody, even Nichola, made posters. Mark got up in assembly Friday and made an impassioned plea to the student body.

"Would you like a new frock for the dance?" Mother asked me. "We could run downtown Saturday morning."

"I haven't time. I'm helping Paul study lines, and there's a rehearsal in the afternoon."

"You're going with Paul Hodge, aren't you?" Mother asked.

I nodded, braced for criticism but she made none, only looked at me searchingly with grave eyes.

Mark was taking Katie to the dance. Paul was taking me. I could tell Katie's feelings on the subject, because she so carefully avoided mentioning it.

Paul and I worked on lines in Gramp's study. Katie wasn't there, being engaged in similar occupation with Mark elsewhere. She came home for lunch, and she and Paul were studiedly polite to one another.

Aunt Tish made a deliberate effort to lift the mood. "Well, Katie, let's see that new dancing cap we've heard so much about."

Katie frowned. "I didn't get it. When I got to the store I only had one dollar in my purse, and I know there should have been four."

"Carelessness," Gram said automatically. Katie shook her head.

"I know I had it. I counted it yesterday. All I could think was somebody must have picked my pocket in the trolley."

Aunt Tish looked puzzled. "Come to think of it, I've missed small sums. I've left loose change in that broken sugar bowl in the kitchen, so I'd have it to tip delivery boys, and then it's gone. And I can't find that little emerald ring Aunt Kate gave me, the one I've promised Nichola."

Katie made a faint sound, quickly stopped. Beside me I could feel Paul breathing hard.

"They'll turn up," Gramp said calmly. "In this house nothing's lost forever. Can I have more soup, Evie?"

AUNT TISH AND KATIE AND PAUL AND I WALKED TO REhearsal together, so there was no chance for private talk.

But I knew what Paul was thinking—or feeling, rather, for his intensity as Shylock rocked the room. Everyone felt it, not knowing its cause, and was impressed. It was nearly dinnertime before we were through. Katie turned to me. "Walk with me, Saranne?" There was a note of appeal in her voice, but over her shoulder I saw a tall figure striding off alone, hands deep in pockets.

"No," I said abruptly. "I'm sorry, Katie, but I just can't."

I had to run to catch up with Paul, and he did not slow down as I fell in beside him.

"Why didn't you go with Miss Know-All?"

"Because I didn't."

"You'd have been better off."

"Don't start that. Paul, will you slow down? I'm out of breath, and we've got to talk."

"Yes, we do." Paul took me by the elbow and steered me to a bench on Grace Church lawn. "I knew this would happen. I tried to warn you, but you wouldn't listen."

"Knew what would happen?"

"You know what."

"All right," I said baldly. "You're determined people will think you took that money, aren't you? Well, nobody's said so. You can't go taking the credit for everything that happens in this neighborhood."

"And you can't go on believing that wishing would change the world!" We were almost shouting at each other, right there in the middle of Tremont Street. Paul took a breath and brushed a strand of hair back from my eyes. "It's been a nice, crazy dream we've had together, but that's all it is, a dream, and that's dangerous, because when you wake up you get hurt. I don't want you hurt. And I don't think you ought to go to the dance with me tonight."

"Paul Hodge," I said when I could manage my voice, "you invited me, and I accepted. And you'd better show up to take me, because I'll be waiting."

I truly didn't know if he would come. Mother and Dad departed to act as chaperones. Seven-thirty came, and eight. I went out on the porch to get away from the sound of Aunt Sadie's voice. It was past eight-thirty when I saw a glimmer through the darkness. The red flare of a cigarette; the squeak of the gate.

"I'm here," I said quietly.

"Hot damn, you really did mean what you said, didn't you?" Paul came up the steps somewhat unsteadily.

"Paul, you've been drinking."

"Got it in one. But then I wasn't expecting to have the pleasure of your company."

"I told you—"

"Yes, I know. I have learned," Paul said carefully, "not to put much faith in promises. But you're different, aren't you? Saranne, do you think you could scare me up a cup of coffee before we go?"

"We don't have to go."

"Yes, we do. Neither of us being there would be infinitely worse than your being there with me. Don't worry, I won't disgrace you."

IT WAS A GOOD THING AUNT TISH HAD NOT FORCED HERSELF
to attend. I knew that as soon as we walked in. The War
was omnipresent. It wasn't just that the dance was a
"benefit for a benefit," as Mr. Moore had put it. The
orchestra that Mark had somehow rounded up played
War songs: "Long, Long Trail," "Tipperary," "I Didn't
Raise My Boy to Be a Soldier." Several Browning
alumni, like Melissa, loyally appeared, and Leslie was
not the only one in uniform among them. And the
newspapers were there. Mark, being a congressman's
son, was copy, and some journalistic spy network had
discovered Aunt Tish's connection with the whole affair.

"Old grad back lending a professional touch for
the War cause, eh?" The grey-haired photographer, who
had just photographed Mark and Katie dancing dreamily ("Getting into mood for romantic roles they will
be playing in two weeks"), chuckled with rueful ad-
miration. "Don't suppose it was you, was it, that sent
Hawkins from the *Journal* about his business? That
would be a story! 'Schuyler III chivalrously comes to
aid of widowed writer.'"

Mark was rocked, but he recovered quickly. "That
would be telling, wouldn't it?" he said with a charming
smile. He eased the photographer over to the side. I
eased, or tried to, Paul toward the floor.

"Let's dance. Please!"

We moved out to the strains of "Long, Long Trail."
"Did you see that look on his face? Trying to figure out
what was what, so he could capitalize on it somehow. I
could kill him."

"Let it go. It's not worth it. *He's* not worth it."

"He'll get something out of it though, you'll see. It's as automatic to him as breathing," Paul said grimly. "He'll have the tale twisted into good publicity in two shakes."

"Then *you* tell it, the way it really happened."

"No. Your aunt's a real lady. She doesn't need any more of that garbage."

And Paul didn't need any more accounts of his being a roughneck, however chivalrous. I tried to put it out of my mind, and I hoped my parents wouldn't notice any lingering smell of liquor on his breath.

The orchestra took a break while we all flocked to the refreshment table. Act natural; smile; don't let Paul see me being conscious of covert glances. Those were only because we were together, and if people didn't like that, it was just too bad. Compliment Katie on her new dress; don't let her see too deeply. Compliment Mark lightly on how well the dance was going. Avoid getting pinned down by him for a tango later.

Mark leaning in toward me, laughing, in that peculiarly intimate way he has. Like throwing a stone in water to watch the ripples. Don't react the way I'd like to; laugh it off; for all our sakes don't let anyone get mad.

Mark turning his tantalizing smile on Paul. "I hear you've been holding out on us, Hodge. I hadn't realized modesty was your strong suit."

Paul, carefully: "I don't know what you mean."

"Oh, come on, now. I mean your gallant rescuing

of our celebrated damsel in distress. Guess the old *Deutsch* courage leaped up again, eh?"

Paul turned furious, betrayed eyes on me.

I scarcely trusted my voice, "Katie, I have to talk to you. *Now.*"

In the girls' room I wheeled on her. "Katie, how could you! When you know how shaken your own sister was, and how badly Paul could have gotten into trouble. You told Mark, and you *laughed* about it, you gave him another weapon to use—"

"Saranne, I was trying to help! Maybe you don't believe that, but I was." Katie swallowed hard; she looked stunned. "It *was* brave of Paul, and you were right, we do emphasize the bad and not the good about Paul Hodge, and so—Oh, rats, Saranne, I was trying to make things better for you, how did I know—"

*Crash* . . . out in the gym. There was a scream. Of one mind, Katie and I pelted out. Were met by Tim. "Oh, thank goodness. You'd both better get over there."

We didn't stop to apologize to the people we pushed aside. I felt as if I were living out a remembered nightmare because I knew so exactly what I'd find.

Mark had made one too many of his barbed witticisms—about Paul's reputation, his chivalry, his honesty? It didn't matter—and Paul had gone for him. They would blame it on Paul's temper, or the drinking . . . but that wasn't all of it, not at all.

Dad was pushing between them, trying to separate them. Dad was sixty-two years old, he didn't belong in the middle of a fight, I saw that writ large on my mother's face. I registered it only vaguely, just as I registered the policeman materializing and moving towards them. Paul was all that was real, Paul who'd taken so much pain that he'd reached the end of his rope and lost control. I flung myself at him with all my strength, wrapping my arms around him to hold him tight. I knew by instinct that Katie, was doing the same with Mark.

Paul didn't even know who I was at first. I pressed myself hard against him, murmuring incoherently, God knows what. And slowly, slowly, I felt the tension oozing out of his body into my own.

"I think it's all right now, Officer Donaldson," I heard my father say.

The policeman shook his head. "Afraid it's not that simple, Mr. Albright. This was a deliberate assault by one student on another, on school property, and he's been drinking. Moore asked us to keep an eye on the place tonight. I was over by the wall, and I saw Hodge launch himself at Schuyler like a mad dog, and Schuyler hadn't even made a move." He turned to Mark. "You want to press charges, son?"

For a wonder, Mark didn't speak. One of those gorgeous eyes was already turning puffy and discolored. Katie had a tight hold of his arm, regardless of who could see. Paul didn't speak either. He won't, I realized with a sinking feeling, and he'll kill me if I say anything about Mark's goading.

"Afraid you'll both have to come down to headquarters so we can straighten this out."

"I'm coming, too," Dad said.

"I'd appreciate that. It shouldn't take long. Sort of goes along with the general reputation, doesn't it?"

Everyone knew who, and what, the policeman meant. And Dad, my civilized elder-statesman father, looked Mark squarely in the eyes and said quietly, "You don't really believe the blame is all one-sided, do you?"

Katie looked sick. I just felt numb. Paul flung me one look—wary, defensive, shamed—and then they were gone. The orchestra, hastily recognizing a cue, launched into boisterous music. Tim grabbed Katie. And I turned and went.

I couldn't go to the police station, that would humiliate Paul. I'd already burned our bridges tonight, publicly proclaiming myself Paul Hodge's girl. I couldn't stay here, surrounded by a blanket of curiosity and well-meaning pity. I walked out not leaving word, not even knowing where I was going until I reached Gram's corner, and the big old tree up and down which Katie and I used to shinny when we were kids.

I hadn't climbed it in years, but I did now, branch by branch, heedless of the damage to my blue silk dress. Instinct stronger than logic drove me towards the one possible source of understanding, until I reached the roof at last and could reach out to knock on the window of Aunt Tish's room.

# VIII

AUNT TISH ASKED NO QUESTIONS, SHE JUST HELD ME WHILE I shook and shook. Afterwards she took me downstairs and made strong coffee and made me drink it. She kept Gram and Gramp out of the kitchen. Gradually, I told her everything.

Letitia's eyes darkened. " 'Inevitable' . . . like a Greek tragedy that's been building up for years."

"But why? Paul thinks now it's anti-German prejudice. But it's more than that, isn't it? It's personal. Not that people are afraid of him because he's dangerous. But the other way round . . . somehow they expect him to be dangerous because they hate him." I ran my fingers through my hair. "I feel as if there's a clue staring me right in the face somewhere, and I just don't see it."

Aunt Tish didn't answer.

The telephone rang. "Yes, she's here," she said into it, and then, "Why don't you all come up? I'll make more coffee."

We ended all gathered round the kitchen table: Gramp, keeping his counsel; Gram, keeping quiet with obvious difficulty; Uncles Peter and Ben, who had been playing poker; Melissa and Leslie and Mother, come from the dance and looking troubled; Katie sliding into the chair beside me, looking as though she'd come apart and tied herself together again in knots. We avoided each other's eyes until she exclaimed, "Oh, hell and damn, kid!" her voice choking, and hugged me hard. The coffeepot circulated, and some leftover cake, but nobody talked much, least of all about what was on our minds.

Then the door opened, and Dad came in. He looked tired; the gap between my parents' ages had been never so apparent. "Well, it's calmed down now. I got Albert Hodge on the phone, and although he's thoroughly convinced now I'm an ambulance-chaser, he agreed to let me represent the boy. So long as it won't cost him anything! Paul's determined he'll pay his legal fees himself, though where he thinks he'll get the money I don't know. Hodge grabs every cent he makes at that after-school job, as board money! And I also called Sherm and made him see that having Mark testify against Paul in an assault case might not be the best publicity in the world for the Schuylers. That's what he's mainly concerned about, of course," Dad said heavily, "the family name. And so, Lord help us at this late date, are the Hodges."

"What's going to happen?"

"Nothing, at the police end. It's a sticky situation with both those families, and they're glad enough to let the school handle it as a disciplinary problem, so long as the school *will*. I'm afraid there's not much doubt Paul will be expelled."

"But they can't *do* that!" I burst out. "Not because

Paul got into just one fight, not even in school hours, and you know he had provocation!"

Dad looked straight at me, not wanting to be cruel. "It's not 'just one fight,'" he said quietly. "I saw the files. Mr. Moore brought them down to the police office, and if he hadn't promised to take action Paul would probably be behind bars right now."

"You mean he showed the police school records about a student!"

"He showed them to *me*," Dad said, still in that quiet voice. "Because I was acting in Paul's interest, and he thought they showed a pattern I should know about."

Uncle Ben nodded. "Behavioral deviance. Incorrigibility." Uncle Ben, the big sharp city lawyer. "Starting with those fires he set when he was eight, I'll bet. And the cat Aunt Kate always insisted he had killed. And the rocks he threw through the windows, starting with his own."

"Grace Alice was always foaming at the mouth to his teachers," Gram said grimly. "Every time they complained to her about him, she moaned how she couldn't do a thing with him either and gave particulars."

I shook my head disbelievingly. "But he didn't even do those things in school."

"There are enough he did," Dad said. "Painting on the kindergarten walls."

"Creativity," Uncle Ben murmured.

"And the tack he put on the seventh-grade teacher's chair. Old Bronson nearly got blood poison."

"How was he to know the old slob never changed his drawers?"

Dad's lip didn't even twitch. "Fire alarm bells pulled. Sand in the inkwells. Constant insolence to teachers. Cutting repeatedly."

"Nothing I didn't do a hundred times," Uncle Ben said, in the same enigmatic tone. "I, and other fellows."

Aunt Tish's tone echoed his. "That's the whole point, isn't it?"

She was looking straight at Uncle Ben. Their eyes locked. Something was being said between them that I didn't understand. But Dad did. And Gramp, and Gram, and Mother.

"He hasn't done anything worse than a million others. Except assault Mark tonight. And everybody thinks MSS III's lily white, but the battering he gives people with that witty tongue can be a lot more vicious than what Paul does with his fists!" I thought Katie would fly at me for that, only she didn't; she just looked sick. "The whole community, even Mr. Moore, thinks he was born bad. Well, what about the way he's been treated? And what is going to happen to him if he is expelled? Then he'll really know there's no use trying! You're pinning a label on him for the rest of his life. 'Guilty without trial.' Guilty of what? Of being born?"

My throat choked; I didn't know where the words had come from. I had stood up, unconsciously; I sat down, for my legs were shaking.

And then Aunt Tish said, "*No.* Saranne's right, she's the only one who's seeing clearly. The sins of the fathers have been visited on the children long enough. We can't change the past, any more than Paul can, but let's be careful of the future. Sidney, if you let that boy get permanently thrown out of school you'll regret it for the rest of your life. We've all got enough sins of omission to contend with, don't let's add more."

"Moore always was an old softy," Gramp said mildly. "He'll settle for a short suspension, once tempers die down. Specially if Ben helps him recall some past history. My sons aren't the only upright citizens around here who have tarnished pasts."

"I'll see," Dad said. "You're right, but we all know right doesn't always cut the ice, and Moore may have to throw the book at Paul even though he doesn't want to. But I'll try."

His words responded to Aunt Tish and Gramp, but he was looking straight at me.

IT WAS THAT LOOK IN EVERYBODY'S EYES THAT WAS THE hardest thing to bear. I was pigeonholed as a vulnerable innocent. They were concerned for me; they pitied me.

I could at least be grateful that my parents didn't pry. Or hover. "Please try," I whispered desperately before I went to bed, and Dad just nodded. When I came downstairs next morning, he was already on the telephone, and Mother and I tiptoed round so as not to interrupt. At church people were gossiping, but the Hodges weren't there, and Katie, Peter, Melissa, and Leslie seemed to have constituted themselves a guard to protect me from the curious. I wondered where Paul was, and *how* Paul was.

In late afternoon Dad and Uncle Ben went out. The phone rang, and it was Katie, inquiring about a school assignment but in reality wanting to know if I was all right. The phone rang, and it was Aunt Tish, wanting to know if we'd come up for Sunday night supper.

"We'd better," Mother said. "Your father will join us, as soon as he gets home."

We had to take Aunt Sadie with us, and that was awful, because she had heard the whole story and she would not shut up. Everybody at Gram's tried to be bright and cheery, which drove me crazy. But there was Nichola, who forgot to be solemn when she tumbled on the floor with her wriggling puppy. Then I would remember Paul's tenderness with Nichola, his instinctive protectiveness toward her, the puppy, Aunt Tish.

Katie came to me. "I talked to Mark on the telephone," she said. "For a long time. He called *me*. If it makes you feel any better, he finally got a real look at MSS III last night, and he feels awful."

A lot of good that did Paul.

Dad and Uncle Ben came in just at twilight, and Dad turned to me with a crooked smile. "It's all right. He's suspended, but he's not expelled. Mr. Moore will call his parents down to school tomorrow, whether they fancy the idea or not, and spell it out. A month's suspension, and if there's one more incident, he's out; but he's got his second chance."

"Why you bother for that hooligan," Aunt Sadie said. "Waste of effort, how you can expect—"

"Sadie," Mother interrupted, loud enough that Aunt Sadie couldn't miss it. "Sadie, that's enough!"

"Dad, does Paul have to wait till tomorrow—?"

Dad's eyes softened. "I guess it wouldn't hurt if you took a load off his mind unofficially."

I couldn't telephone him, with all those flapping ears. And I knew Paul would not call me. Not after he'd promised he'd not disgrace me. So I walked out before I could lose my courage. But it wasn't Paul who came to the Hodges' door, it was Mr. Hodge.

He had been drinking, and my new spring shoes felt weighted with cement. No, Paul wasn't home; he didn't know where he was; he dang well didn't care. Be better for everybody if he never showed up. I was Sid Albright's kid, wasn't I; what was I doing mixed up with the lousy bastard.

I threw caution to the winds. "Tell Paul it's all right, he doesn't have to worry. He's not expelled, only suspended for a month. Everything's going to be all right."

"Don't see how you can say that," Mr. Hodge mumbled truculently. "Hasn't been all right since the brat was born. Or before that. OK, you want to take a chance with him, no skin off my nose, just be careful you don't get caught in history repeating."

The door slammed.

I went home numbly.

Monday was rainy. Mr. Moore tried all morning to reach Paul on the telephone and could not, and the Hodges flatly refused to appear. I heard all this along the grapevine.

There was rehearsal. The air was filled with everyone's private and personal confrontations, and Tish twisted all those separate pulsing chords into the texture of the play. But halfway through she looked at me and said quietly, "Saranne, go home," and I did.

It hadn't dawned on me until I let myself into the still house what Paul's suspension was going to do to Shylock. A month. The play was well within that time. Students weren't allowed to participate in any school activities while they were suspended. The phone rang and I went to answer it.

"Saranne?"

"Paul? Where are you?"

"Never mind. Can you get out without anybody knowing where?"

"*Now?* Yes, Mother's at Suffrage League. Paul, what—"

"Meet me under the porch of your uncle's house in ten minutes. He won't be home at this hour. Please, Saranne, I need you." He rang off.

I grabbed my sweater and dashed off. Fast as I was, Paul was there before me. I could see his footprints in the spongy ground beside the lilacs. I bent down by the dark cave-opening in the broken lattice, and Paul's hands reached out to pull me in.

He was lying on the ground, and I dropped down beside him. "What hap—" I started to say, and then I gasped, staring at his face. Even in the dimness I could see the livid stripe that ran across his cheek. "Paul, *how?*"

"How do you think?" Paul said harshly. "The Old

Man. Because I slugged Mark. Because his sleep last night was disturbed. Because I disgraced the glorious name of Hodge and got suspended again."

"Didn't you tell him your side of it?"

Paul looked at me as if I were very stupid. "Nobody tells him anything. And there's only one side. His." His fists clenched; unclenched. "He's never once asked my version of a thing. He may be a dumb Hun, but not too dumb to know I'm the one to blame. He just pulled out his belt and started swinging. I ducked, and—" After a moment he went on in a lower voice. "I just got out of there. If I hadn't, I don't know what I'd . . . I swear, Saranne, I'm scared of what I may do to him some day."

"But you didn't," I said. "You walked out without letting your temper blow. That must mean something."

"Maybe," Paul said ambiguously.

Blood was oozing along the edge of the bruise where the belt had struck him. I searched my pockets for a handkerchief. "What are you going to do now?" I asked, dabbing.

"I don't know. I've got to get away from here. Saranne, can you lend me some money? I hate to ask, but I'll pay it all back."

"Paul Hodge, you can't run away! That would only make things worse, once your father found you."

Paul looked at me. "Do you honestly think he'd bother looking?"

The reality of that hit me like a blow, and so did the expression in Paul's eyes. They were so bitter, and so angry . . . and so vulnerable. Involuntarily, I reached out both hands toward his face. And then he was kissing me, but differently, not gently as he had the time before. And then we were lying in each other's arms, and he was holding me. A part of me wanted to keep him there, protected from all harm. A part of me was afraid.

All at once, in confusion and shame, I was pulling myself away. "Paul, please . . . no . . . ."

Almost I could not get free and did not want to. It was Paul who suddenly thrust me from him roughly. "You're like a mirage I keep believing in, and shouldn't. Because I'll hurt you, just like I do me. Why in God's name did you have to come here?"

"Because you asked me to," I said simply.

"You shouldn't have. Everybody could have told you that. You should have listened." Paul was breathing hard. " 'Sarah Anne Albright,' " he mimicked savagely, " 'and that wild—' . . . why the hell did we start something we can't finish?"

We stared at each other in a silence that was charged with all the things we dared not say.

And then a voice, a very quiet, noncommittal voice, was saying, "Come out of there, both of you, right away." Aunt Tish's voice.

We crawled out. Paul went first; but he held out his hand to help me.

Aunt Tish led the way into the house, unlocking the door in silence. It was dark inside. She lit a lamp and looked at us and all at once I was acutely conscious of our state. Paul's head went up in the old bravado.

"It wasn't what you were thinking—"

I flushed scarlet, remembering, but Aunt Tish just gave him a level look. "How can you know what I'm thinking? I'm not Miss Sadie, nor your mother. Nor mine, if it comes to that." Her eyes flicked over Paul's bruised face, but she made no comment, just went to the kitchen and returned with milk and cake and a wet cloth with which she began to sponge the cut. "Paul, sit down. I can reach you better. Don't worry about the chair, I can clean the mud off after."

She put iodine on the cut, and Paul flinched, but didn't make a sound. It was I who had to press my knuckles against my mouth.

When she was finished she said, flatly, "You can go now. I won't presume to tell you what to do. If you're wise, Paul, you'll go back home, and if you're even wiser you'll get there after your father's left for Lodge tonight. By the time he gets back it will be midnight, and you'll be asleep." She didn't add, *and he'll be too drunk to notice.* "And in future, don't try lying under the porch. The ground's too damp."

Paul, flushing, strode to the door, then turned. "May I see you home?" he asked me quietly.

But I was shaking too much. "I'd like to stay with Aunt Tish awhile . . . if that's all right."

Tish nodded, and after a moment Paul said gently, "That's a good idea."

"Are you going home?"

"I don't know."

"Paul—call me. Please."

He didn't answer, just slipped out. Aunt Tish looked at me, and I wondered how I ever could have thought her eyes were shuttered.

"Aren't you going to give me the family lecture?" I burst out. "Don't you want to know what a nice girl like me was doing—"

"Why should I?" Letitia asked quietly. "*You* know what you were doing, and why. I won't insult you by saying you're too young for what you're feeling."

"Aren't you even going to ask about Paul's face?" I said, in a considerably smaller voice.

"I don't have to. I've seen belt marks before." Letitia's hand rested for a moment on my shoulder. "Come on, let's go to Gram's. Go up the back way and put on my kimono. Your dress is clammy with mud and you'll get a chill."

We went in Gram's back door, and I didn't see Katie till I'd come back down, and she asked no questions. It was Aunt Tish who called Mother to say I'd stay for dinner, and we had a cozy kimono supper for my grandparents were down at night school and neither Melissa nor Peter were home. I stayed over, and shared the bed with Katie, and when I cried in the night she didn't even pry, just wrapped her arms around me and held me until my tears were gone.

SUSPENDED. IN LIMBO. IT SEEMED SUCH AN APPROPRIATE word, as if Paul were swinging by a thread above a void. The play felt suspended, too. We waited in jittery silence for fifteen minutes the next afternoon until Aunt Tish arrived, taut-lipped.

"I've just seen Mr. Moore. We have no Shylock."

On the desk the costume fabrics purchased from the dance proceeds jeered at us mockingly.

"Maybe—" Mark spoke with difficulty, stopped, began again. "Maybe it's better that we stop. We started all wrong, for all wrong reasons."

Nobody spoke. I saw Katie's hand touch his, tentatively, and his tighten round it.

I felt, suddenly, very lonely.

Aunt Tish was staring at Mark, or through him—what she was seeing I could not say, but I knew it shook her.

"You are right," she said slowly. "But not about it being better if we stop. We can't give up—not if there's any chance at all. Especially not when that's one more thing for which a person could be blamed unfairly." She rose abruptly. "We'll be in touch. No rehearsal today. I have some unfinished business to attend to."

We dispersed. Katie and I did not go together; she lingered, watching Mark, and I knew that I did not belong. I walked home to find Aunt Sadie holding forth again. Everything in me screamed to get away, but I had to be there just in case Paul called. I was afraid he would not, but I knew I must wait, must not make the move, must leave the choice to him.

It was close to dinnertime when the phone did ring.

"Saranne?"

"Are you all right?"

"Yes. I need to see you. Please."

We met at Uncle Ben's house, that borrowed haven, for everywhere else there were too many eyes and ears. We sat on the porch, our knees not even touching, and neither of us spoke.

"I had to see you," Paul said at last. "I wanted so much to keep you out of this mess. You shouldn't be involved with me."

"But I am involved," I said simply.

"I'm out of the play. Another way I've loused things up for you and your aunt."

"I know. And it's not important."

Paul grinned raggedly. "You know something? I didn't realize, but I really wanted to play that crazy old guy." He tried to laugh, but that was a mistake. I didn't even try to talk. I just reached over and held him tightly.

After a while Aunt Tish came up the walk. We didn't move, and she just smiled faintly and sat down beside us in a wicker chair. She looked tired.

"Well, there's one less thing for you to feel burdened by. The play won't be cancelled."

"Who's going to play Shylock."

"Kenneth Latham." She unpinned her hat and laid it on her lap, methodically, as we both straightened. "He was the one person I could think of who'd be able to step in and do it. It wouldn't have been right for me not to ask him just to spare my feelings. So I asked him."

"And he said yes?"

She nodded briefly. "It's not really his type of part, but he can do it. I think he really wanted to help . . .

us . . . out." She sounded faintly surprised, and also troubled. "I'll talk to Mr. Moore and see if we can postpone the production a week or two, so Kenneth can rehearse."

It wouldn't have done any good suggesting we postpone the play so Paul could be in it after his suspension. One of the conditions to his coming back to school at all was that he be there only for classes during the rest of this school year.

But it wasn't Paul Aunt Tish was thinking about at the moment, I could tell. She shook herself slightly. "Nichola must be worrying about where I was. Are you two joining us at the Sterling Free Lunch Counter?"

We seemed to be boarding at Gram's a great deal these days.

THE PLAY WAS POSTPONED, AND PAUL WAS NO LONGER IN it, and Mr. Latham was. It made a difference, just as Aunt Tish's coming had. For one thing, his needing time to rehearse gave the cast an extra two weeks. For another, he came up with the solution to our dire need for help with sets, costumes, lights.

"Tish and I are in this already. Why not rope in all the Browning alumni who are around? You want something that will be a drawing card for War relief."

Overnight, we had a pool of experienced talent, onstage and off. We also had a tremendous promotional gimmick on which Mark seized brilliantly. But the whole feeling of the show had changed. It was not ours, any more.

Aunt Tish went up in Gram's attic and rummaged through trunks. "I'm sure the original Browning costumes were stored here somewhere." She drew out a Renaissance gown with a high-waisted crimson velvet bodice, its heavy white satin skirt pearl-encrusted. "I wore it as Juliet. This was her wedding gown. See, Kenneth had this doublet and cloak to match." She fingered the lilac gauze tenderly, a faraway expression in her eyes. Then, with an effort, she turned back to me.

"What have you found, our old Browning Literary Quarterlies? Take them along, too."

She carried Juliet's gown downstairs for Katie to try, but she did not take Romeo's lavender silks for Mark.

I told Paul about the costumes, as I told him all about rehearsals—because he wished to hear it. He wasn't allowed to set foot near them himself.

"But I'll come to the play," he promised. "That's open to the public. They can't keep me out."

"You don't have to." I knew what it would cost him to run the gamut of the neighborhood's speculative eyes.

"I want to. I don't know who I'm trying to prove something to, or what, but I have to. Besides, I want to see it."

Something had happened in Paul; something had turned him clear around. It made me ache, seeing it, knowing how many people in West Farms believed the leopard could not change his spots. All of a sudden, Paul could let it show that people's good opinion mattered to him . . . that he was beginning to believe it was possible for him to have it, because of Aunt Tish, and Dad, and me.

I felt like a commuter between worlds as May came in. Home was the bleak oppressiveness of Aunt Sadie's presence. Then there was school, where the play was progressing, although it really didn't matter to me any more. And there was the world of Uncle Ben's house and Paul.

Aunt Tish had performed the transformation and had moved in, at least partly because Mr. Latham had made her. He had taken rooms at an apartment hotel, and he would not take no for an answer to his offers of transportation and assistance. "Tish, you know living under the same roof with your mother leads to fire-works. Nichola needs a home that seems familiar." He was fond of Nichola, that showed early, and Nichola was polite to him, but it was Paul she adored. And she saw Paul, even more often, once they'd moved.

Entering that house was like entering an enchanted space, a cross between Charles Dickens and William Shakespeare and something even earlier. Letitia had had the woodwork painted deep soft shades—"the closest substitute I could get for old oak paneling"—and all her colors melted deliciously into one another. Apricot, coral, aqua, olive green. All Aunt Tish's chairs and sofas were deeply comfortable. They invited you to put your feet up and settle in, and only afterwards did you realize that the upholstery was velvet, that the plain heavy drapes, which were drawn as soon as darkness fell, were of satin. That unmistakable foreign touch was everywhere—in the brass fire fenders, the brass hanging plaques upon the chimneys, the tapestries and toast rack and hot water kettle.

Aunt Tish had not let anyone see it till it was all arranged. Our expressions must have told her our delight, but it was Nichola's reaction she was watching for. First astonished, and then a look of intense relief and recognition. "Familiar territory," Paul murmured, and I nodded. And then, suddenly, a wave of sheer horror swept over her. She swung round on Aunt Tish, stark and accusing.

"We're not going Home, are we? We're not ever going Home! You promised!"

"Darling, we've been over this a hundred times." Tish knelt to her. "We're going to live here till the War is over. But we'll be able to go back to England then."

"No! This isn't home. I want my own home. I want my Papa."

I marveled at the quietness and deliberation of Aunt Tish's tone, because her mouth was shaking. "Oh, darling, I know. We both want him. But Nikki dear, you have to face it. He isn't coming back. He can't. He's dead."

"No! You're lying, because you don't want to go Home. I hate you! I won't believe you, ever!" It was Paul she ran to, Paul who caught her and scooped her up and rocked her. Tish held her hands out to Mr.

Latham, blindly, and he took them, and I knew I was extraneous and crept away.

PAUL AND I SPENT AS MUCH TIME AS WE COULD AT THE house, and not for Nichola's sake alone.

"I hardly see you any more," Katie said, a trifle sadly. I knew she understood, although I could feel her watching me with that concerned look that both touched and rankled. Dad and Mother had it, too. Once the play was over, I'd have more time for everyone, I told myself. And soon after the play was over, Paul would be back in school. Meanwhile I was dividing myself between my duties as Aunt Tish's assistant and Paul. I couldn't breathe it, but I was getting sick and tired of that everlasting play.

Paul was helping, almost as a penance, in every way he could. He was free in the daytime, so he took posters round. (Mr. Moore pretended not to know.) He helped load borrowed furniture in wagons, though he couldn't do the unloading on school grounds. He and Uncle Peter went around in Uncle Ben's auto, collecting door prizes Uncle Ben had seduced from local merchants, and they hung the banner advertising the play across Tremont Street.

"He reminds me of Mary," Aunt Tish murmured one evening, watching him putting raffle books together.

Uncle Ben nodded. "The same intense energy, focused so doggedly on spitting in everybody's eye, that can do so much good once it's channeled."

A new Mary Hayes picture opened in the neighborhood, but Paul did not suggest we go. It was partly not wanting to call attention to us, and partly lack of money. "Don't you ever see your sister?" I asked Paul, and he shook his head."

"Not in years. She writes me, though, once in a while, and she sends me things. Birthdays and Christmas. She lives across the river in Fort Lee."

"Doesn't she ever come back?"

"Can you blame her?" Paul retorted bluntly. "She was lucky. *She* got away." He was silent for a moment. "I was a little kid, but I can still remember the row. It was awful. She'd just started making movies, and she came home late one night, and Dad was roaring drunk. He called her a scarlet woman and a lot worse garbage, and she packed her bags and just cleared out."

"It was the best thing that ever happened to Mary," Aunt Tish said when I relayed this conversation. "She was like a—a creature from another planet, here. What was good for the rest of us almost destroyed her. She was in the wrong soil, especially at home."

"Sometimes I'm afraid that's true for Paul, as well."

"Yes. One of the hardest things to bear, isn't it, is having to sit on your hands when you don't have the right to do transplanting. And to accept . . . once you've found your own right soil . . . that some of those you most love would not thrive in it." I thought at first that she meant Nichola, and then I saw a certain expression in her eyes, and it struck me that she was thinking of something much further back. And I remembered the family assumption that there had been an understanding once between her and Mr. Latham . . . until she went to England and felt so suddenly at home there and did not come back.

The Browning Society Members and Alumni Gala War Relief Production was creating great excitement. We were deluged with ticket orders, and Mark was jubilant. It didn't even rankle him that the entry of the Old Grads had completely stolen his own thunder. "Now if we could just hit our goal of one thousand dollars for Liberty Loan through the raffle!"

It was a fantastic goal for a school group to attempt, but we were already close.

The Friday of the first performance was hot and misty. Paul was waiting for me on Uncle Ben's porch when I came there from school. He was still sticking to his vow to attend the play, and I wouldn't let him go through that alone.

"I have to be there early to help with makeup. I'll meet you in the auditorium," I told him. "I'll save seats. Third row center."

"How's the raffle going?"

"We just might make it. Everybody'd love to announce that from the stage tonight."

Paul stood up restlessly. "You've still got raffle tickets around here, haven't you? I know a great stop I'll bet nobody's tried."

"Where?"

"Corner by O'Rourke's Saloon. It's payday," Paul

said wryly. "All the men coming off the day shift at the freight yards will be ready to blow their money."

THE MEN WITH THEIR LUNCH PAILS AND OVERALLS WERE even more patriotic with their loose change than the dowagers had been in Aunt Sadie's part of town.

Paul looked at me. "It's getting late. Isn't it time you quit?"

"Can't we wait fifteen minutes more?"

"It's clouding up. I think we're in for it finally," Paul said. And then, "Oh, dang!"

Thunder crackled, and the heavens opened. The rain plastered my clothes against my skin.

"Inside," Paul shouted. We dove into the close steamy warmth of the saloon.

"Here, kids!" We were engulfed with help. Chairs were pushed forward, tablecloths wrapped around us like blankets, mugs of coffee thrust into our hands. We made a lot more raffle sales, too.

"I'll see if O'Rourke will let me phone your father," Paul said. "Maybe he can come pick you up in the auto. It's not going to let up for a while."

My soaking hair was half-blinding me. I nodded. And then, through a veil of hair, my eyes encountered a pair of shiny black shoes. My gaze traveled, in horrified fascination, up dark blue trousers, an official tunic. "Good grief," said Officer Donaldson's voice. "What are you kids doing here?"

It was against the law, it seemed, for us to be soliciting for a raffle in a public place without a permit.

It was wrong, of course, for kids to be in a saloon at all. And even more so for *me* to be there with *a boy like that,* his tone implied.

"It's my fault," I blurted out hastily, before Paul could speak. "I was selling for the raffle and got caught in the thunderstorm, and just—came in here. I didn't know about the permit." I had less to lose than Paul; he wasn't supposed to be involved in school affairs at all, and if his pride was hurt this time it was just too bad. "Paul just ran into me and was looking after me because I got wet."

Paul looked outraged. Mr. O'Rourke, comprehending, put his hand on Paul's arm. "Keep your lip buttoned, kid," he counseled.

Paul ignored him. "Mr. Donaldson, will you see that Saranne gets home? I'll wait here with Mr. O'Rourke, if you want me to, but get her out of here."

I had the honor of riding home in a paddy wagon, and Aunt Sadie aged ten years.

Mother ignored her, just hustled me into the bathtub and brought me supper, and I talked to her while I ate and soaked, like Madame DuBarry.

"I'll tell your father. I wouldn't worry," Mother said. "This won't amount to a hill of beans, and Sidney will handle it."

She buttoned me into my rose Easter silk, and Dad drove me to the school.

*The Merchant of Venice* was a beautiful production, particularly because of the Old Grad angle. Aunt Tish directing at the school in which she'd got her start

. . . Kenneth Latham the publisher playing Shylock . . . the splendor of sets and costumes. *Everybody* came. There was talk, as early as half an hour before the curtain rose, of doing an extra third night performance because the house was packed.

Katie was astonishing, even to me who had seen her at rehearsal. And Mr. Latham was very good; I could picture him, in my mind's eyes, as Romeo with Aunt Tish all those years ago. But for me, the play was ghostlike, because it didn't have that special real-life quality that Paul's Shylock had brought it. And Paul didn't sit beside me, because he wasn't there.

He didn't come. The seat in the third row beside me stayed empty through the first act, the second, and I kept my head up and kept on smiling, because I didn't want to give any of the vultures fuel for their fires.

It was after the play, when all of us were milling around backstage with congratulations, that Mr. Moore approached me. "Saranne, there's a private telephone call for you in my office."

"I didn't want you to think I stood you up." Paul's voice sounded strained and faraway.

"Paul, where *are* you?"

"At the police station. I'm allowed one call, and I didn't want to use it earlier and spoil your evening. But I wanted to be sure you didn't think I'd just not come."

"Never mind that. What's happened? Tell me."

"What do you think?" Paul said in that old bitter, self-condemning tone. "This time I didn't manage to walk out first. They say I tried to kill my father."

# May

# IX

THE POLICE STATION WAS WHITE-LIT AND BLEAK. FOR THE
rest of my life, I thought, I'm going to remember the
shape and look of these mahogany chairs, the speckled
fly-paper, the posters on the wall.

Dad had brought me. He hadn't even bothered suggesting I not come.

"I'm sorry, Sidney," the desk sergeant said. "I know
you like the boy. But it's really serious this time."

"What happened?" Dad asked calmly.

"Regular street fight. The old man was likkered
up, of course, but the boy was not. He swung at his old
man with the fireplace poker. Laid him out cold, with
a nasty concussion and a broken jaw. It's a wonder it
wasn't a whole lot worse. I'll say this for the boy, when
he realized what he'd done he called us and stayed with
him till we got there with an ambulance; he didn't cut
and run."

"That should mean something."

The sergeant shook his head. "Not enough, considering the past history and the fact that he was on probation. *And* the fact that his father's already signed an assault charge against him. Claims the boy's a danger to himself and others, and he's afraid to have him around. Maybe you can get the boy to tell what started it. We can't."

They brought Paul in, and I went sick with shock. It wasn't the torn shirt and bruises—Paul moved like a character in a horror serial at the movies. He wouldn't look at us at all. He wouldn't answer Dad's careful questions.

"It doesn't matter. Nothing matters." That was all he'd say.

"That's the way he's been ever since he got here," the sergeant said.

"It does matter to a lot of us," Dad said. "Me. Tish. Saranne." He tried again. "Saranne's here, Paul. Would you talk to her?"

Paul jerked involuntarily. "I don't want her here."

*"But I do,"* I said loudly, and I walked across and made him face me. I took his hands, as Mr. Latham had Aunt Tish's, and led him across the room to an empty bench. The sergeant started to protest; my father raised an authoritative hand to stop him.

Paul started to shake. "Oh, God, Saranne, I didn't want you to see me here."

"What happened? Paul, you've got to tell me."

Painfully, he groped for words. "This afternoon

. . . Mr. Donaldson said he wouldn't bring charges, but he insisted that he personally escort me home. I knew what would happen. And it did."

"Your father blew up about it?"

"What do you think?" Paul said flatly. "Rotten kid, disgrace to the family, the whole song and dance. And him so plastered already he could barely get the words out straight."

"But why—you've heard it all before. Why this time did you—"

"I *told* you I was afraid this would happen." Paul stopped. "He kept coming at me, and coming at me, like something was *making* him drive me to fight. I kept backing away, till he had me by the fireplace, and he kept coming. . . . That's why I picked up the poker, to hold him off, so he wouldn't grab at me. So I wouldn't swing. He's right, I *am* dangerous. 'Born bad,' it's like I've got a devil inside me somewhere that I can't control."

"But you *do* control it, more and more." I caught my breath. "Something was different this time, wasn't it? What was it? Tell me."

"No."

"*Tell* me."

"It was because you were there," Paul said, so quietly. "He said . . . wasn't it bad enough that I was rotten—did I have to drag you down, too. And then he started to laugh . . . he wanted to know, were you—putting out—pulling the wool over your father's eyes, too. He kept shouting something crazy about history repeating. And all I could hear was what I'd done to you, touching your life, and the way he was—cheapening you, and I just . . . swung."

I WENT BACK TO MY FATHER AND TOLD HIM WHAT PAUL had said. I had to speak carefully, because now I too was shaking. I stood, hands locked together, as Paul was taken away, and paperwork formalities were completed, and then Dad very gently led me out to the car.

We rode home in silence. "Why didn't you get him out?" I burst out once, and Dad said, "Because he refused bail. He's afraid to be out. He's starting to believe those things about himself, now . . . and besides, the fact that his own father brought the charge makes it more serious."

By morning, everybody knew. Aunt Tish walked in, white-faced, while we were at breakfast, and soon after Mr. Latham and Katie arrived too. "I'm trying to keep Nichola from finding out. She adores him so," Aunt Tish said. "Sidney, what happens now?"

"We try to build the best case for him we can. Self-defense, or justification."

"Don't know why you're all so shocked," Aunt Sadie sniffed. "You can't make a silk purse out of a sow's ear. Bad blood. You'd've been better off tending your own daughter, 'stead of letting her mix with him. You want history repeating on your hands?"

I started to shake. Katie squeezed my hand hard. Dad looked his sister squarely in the eyes. "One more word like that, *ever*, Sadie," he said quietly, "and I'll pack you off to an old people's home, I swear to God."

THERE WAS ANOTHER PERFORMANCE OF THE PLAY THAT night and then *that* was over. Backstage, and at the party later, there was gossip about the Hodge case. "The Hodge case," that's what it was already being called, as though Paul and his father were specimens under a microscope, not people at all.

And I, hadn't I really pinned a label on Paul as well? Paul, the sensitive, the mistreated, the misunderstood. I loved him, I believed in him . . . but had I really reached out to him, to *him*, at all? Or had I been taking unto myself the old Tish Sterling label, *"sensitive champion of the waifs and strays,"* because I felt so suffocated by other tags: Katie's shadow, Mother's daughter, *Saranne Albright, that nice little girl.*

Suddenly Aunt Tish sat down beside me. "Do you ever have a feeling," she murmured, "that you're suddenly watching people under a truth-glass, with all their inner parts exposed, not the way you've seen them before at all?"

I glanced at her, startled, and she sighed. "I thought you might. My grandfather told me once it meant that for a few minutes we're seeing through God's eyes. It happens to creative people more than most, but it hits us all, I guess, when crisis strikes."

"I feel so ashamed," I murmured, and she nodded.

"You'll get over it. And you're not alone, if that's

any comfort. It can help you, if you'll let it. And I just hope," she added, "that the phenomenon happens to enough people for it to do some good for Paul."

Dad tried again to get Paul out on bail. He even offered to put the money up himself. But Paul refused flatly.

"If only Paul hadn't used a weapon," Dad kept saying. "That's what makes the whole situation so bad."

"He only picked the poker up to defend himself! He was afraid!"

"Which was he more afraid of, his father or himself?" Dad asked, and my eyes fell. "If he'd swung with his fists, it might not have been so bad. Paul can't prove he picked the thing up to hold his father off. I'm afraid he's even starting to doubt it now himself. And I'm also afraid there will be a lot of witnesses to testify that this is just one of a long string of progressively more anti-social acts. The DA's under pressure. We can't have things like this happen in our nice neighborhood." Dad sounded bitter, and he sounded old.

Mr. Hodge was still in the hospital. It was reputed that Mr. Schuyler was helping him with medical bills. "A gracious gesture to a constituent," Katie said sardonically. "He's also letting it be known how deeply grieved he feels that he exercised misguided kindness in not bringing charges when this obviously disturbed lad assaulted his own son."

"How come you're so sarcastic these days about Mark's father?"

Katie looked at me. "Because he *is* Mark's father

and never lets him forget it. You think that's easy for him?"

This conversation took place while Katie and I were studying in my room. Final exams were upon us, and she had come to spend the night. In a weird way, we welcomed the scholastic pressure, for it occupied our minds.

"I've been pretty rotten to you about Paul, haven't I? I'm sorry." Katie didn't look up over the top of her chemistry book. "You may not believe me, but I really do hope he gets out of this all right."

"I know you do."

"It's too bad one of us can't do a Portia and rush in to save the day." And then, "Bad joke. Sorry."

Downstairs, the doorbell rang.

"I'll have to go. Dad and Mother are out." I pulled my kimono tight and went downstairs with Katie trailing after.

Mark Schermerhorn Schuyler III stood on the porch.

For a minute I just gaped at him. Then he said, "May I come in?" in an oddly subdued voice, and I said, "Of course," and led the way to the parlor, painfully conscious that I was in my robe. Katie came with us, belting hers like armor, and we sat down in an awkward, self-conscious triangle.

Mark cleared his throat. "I've been walking around in the dark, trying to figure out what I should do, and I finally realized I didn't have any choice. And I knew I had to talk to you."

"Want me to go?" Katie asked in a dry voice.

"No. You'd find out anyway, and I'd rather you heard it from me, especially because a lot of what I've been thinking stemmed from things you've said."

"Mark," I said, striving for the light touch, "do you suppose you could let us in on what you're talking about?"

"I've been subpoenaed as a witness against Paul. To testify as an innocent victim of his unmotivated violence."

Neither Katie nor I found anything to say.

"My dad's been talking to me about it," Mark went on after a pause. "I couldn't believe he'd spare me this much time when he has an election coming up! He keeps harping on all the reasons Hodge should be locked up and telling me how wise I've been to recognize that fact and to 'instinctively seize on opportunities to keep the lad suppressed and in control.' He's so proud of me; he keeps saying he's known all along I had it in me, I'm a chip off the old block, I have a born aptitude for politics." He turned to Katie. "Only I keep hearing *your* voice, telling me that my 'anticipating' had been prejudice, that 'instinctiveness' was plain cold-blooded opportunism."

I stared at Katie, astounded. She wasn't looking at me; she had dropped her eyes.

"I thought a lot about what you said to me, that night at the dance. How words could be used as weapons, just like fists. And when you turned around and walked out on me when I pleaded innocent . . ." Mark shook his head. "That got to me. I never thought a girl would turn her back on the Schuyler charm, especially when I was behaving exactly as I'd been taught. But when I tried to talk about it with my father—he didn't even hear me. He didn't want to know any extenuating factors for Paul, at all. I felt as if I were looking in a mirror, and seeing myself. I've always wanted to see my father's image in my mirror, but not like that."

There was a soft rustle. Katie had crossed over to sit beside Mark on the sofa.

After a time, he went on. "I guess I knew, then, which way things were heading. But it wasn't till this afternoon, when the subpoena came, that the pieces added up. Dad kept saying how he knew he could count on me, that my testimony would be a public service for the community, and I must be sure not to muddle the evidence by dragging in irrelevant ideas. He clapped me on the back. Just the way he treats the ward captains down at the precinct house when he wants a favor; and they hustle to earn their crumbs of recognition, poor slobs, just the way I always have."

"Do you mean," I asked slowly, "that he wants you to slant your testimony to make Paul look guilty even if you think it's not his fault?"

"Got it in one," Mark said. Then his face colored. "You have to understand . . . Dad sincerely believes that he's doing what is best, that Paul *is* unredeemable, just as I thought. Only I can't go back to seeing things so black and white any more."

"What are you going to do?" I asked. Mark shrugged.

"I don't know. I *have* to testify. I'll tell the story to give Hodge the benefit of the doubt as much as possible. But as Dad says, any speculations on my part as to pressures and unconscious goadings are going to sound like so much sophomoric drivel." He looked at me. "I went down to the jail, after the subpoena came. I wanted Hodge to know I wasn't testifying willingly. But he wouldn't see me. Not that I blame him. So will you tell him for me?"

"He won't see me, either." I tried to say it as simply as I could. I was not too successful. There was another long stillness, then Mark slapped his hand against his leg.

"If only some of this had gotten through my thick Dutch head sooner! If only I'd listened to you, Saranne, when you stood up for him way back last winter. But I didn't believe you could size up Paul better than I could. I told myself you were lying or deluded, because for some insane reason you'd fallen for him. I guess what I couldn't take was the notion you could fall for anything but the Schuyler charm," he said bitterly. "And when you kept on sticking up for him . . . it did get through to me that if somebody like you stood by him, there had to be more to him than the surface showed, regardless of the evidence. Even if he *had* filched Katie's necklace."

"It never has turned up," Katie said with a curious reluctance.

"He didn't take it."

There was a queer little silence. Mark and Katie

looked at each other. "Saranne," Katie said gently, "there have been other things that disappeared. Money, and—and that little emerald ring that was left for Nichola. From our house, and from Tish's, too, times when Paul's been there. You can't provide alibis for him every minute of all those times. Oh, Saranne, I didn't want you to have to know, but you'd better face that he could have taken them, even if he's been railroaded on the other charges."

"I won't believe it," I said stubbornly.

"If those things would just turn up somewhere Paul couldn't possibly have put them," Katie said doggedly. "There has to be some logical explanation."

"We can look for them. That's one thing we *can* do. Because I guarantee they're going to get dragged in at the trial. Dad told me." Mark rose. "Saranne, will you tell your father about all this? Maybe he can find some way to keep the DA from forcing me into corners when I'm on the witness stand."

THERE WERE THREE MORE DAYS OF SCHOOL, AND SIX MORE till the beginning of Paul's trial.

Mr. Hodge came home from the hospital, his head bandaged and his arm in a sling. He was making it very clear that he didn't want Paul back in his house, ever; that he was afraid of what Paul might do next. "No good, knew it would turn out this way, ungrateful for all we've done for him," was the burden of his song.

"Does it occur to you," Mark asked me and Katie, "that there's something queer there? Grateful for what, that they brought him up? What was he supposed to do, pay room and board? My old man heaps on a heavy load of expectations, and the responsibility of being a Schuyler, but he never talks of gratitude. And I've never heard of anything the Hodges gave him to be grateful for."

"Your parents expected perfection. His expected just the opposite."

"That's exactly what I mean. Why?"

"Mama's been known to come down pretty hard about ungrateful kids," Katie said. "But you're right, something does seem fishy."

Had I always, deep down, had this suspicion where Paul was concerned—that there was something hidden, something that would explain everything, but that was concealed by a conspiracy of silence. Why had Aunt Tish, who had known Paul only as a baby, reacted to him as she had when they first met?

I asked Mother, and she just said, "You're imagining things. Tish has known the Hodges all her life. She and Ben were sort of friends of Mary Lou—I mean Mary Hayes. Naturally she'd be interested."

"That's just it. It's the people who've known the Hodges who expect the worst from Paul. And they never want to talk about it. Why?"

Mother retreated into her parental voice. "Whatever you're noticing—if there *is* anything to notice—it couldn't possibly have any bearing on Paul's case. Don't you think Paul could be hurt if you poke around?"

"When you stir up a muddy pond, you got to cope with what comes floating up," was Gramp's cryptic response to the same question.

They neither of them gave a flat-out denial to my suggestion that there was something murky to be stirred up. Was that because neither of them were very good at lying?

Finding out what was hidden—finding *something* to vindicate Paul—was becoming an obsession with me.

We couldn't do anything till school was out. Mark, especially, had to concentrate on exams because he was graduating and would be attending NYU next year. But when we got out of school at noon on Friday, we went to Katie's house, she and Mark and I. Mark's organizational skill was a blessing, for we planned to search Gram's house from top to bottom. We worked our way methodically, room by room, checking every possible place anything could have been concealed, or blown, or fallen. But at the end of three hot, trying hours we were forced to concede defeat.

"The little house next." Katie rubbed a grimy arm across her face. Our search of the cellar had revealed cobwebs, to Gram's annoyance.

We went through the yards and looked under the porch, where Paul and I had met. Aunt Tish came to meet us. "I'm trying to get Nichola down to the library. I used to love it there when I was small. And I'd rather she not find out what this is all about. She's terribly upset that Paul hasn't come to see her lately, and if she finds out the truth about him—"

"What truth?" I stared at her, furiously blinking back tears. "Don't tell me you've turned against him, too!"

"Oh, my dear, to recognize the possibility of weakness, or wrongdoing, in someone is not necessarily to turn against him." She put her hand on my shoulder, and when I involuntarily drew back she let it fall. "You don't understand that yet, do you? I hope you won't have to." She shook her head, sounding sad, and led the way into the house.

Nichola was in the hall. She measured Mark with that disconcertingly cool gaze of hers and asked me accusingly, "Why didn't you bring Paul?"

"Paul's away. He can't come for a while. Won't I do in the meantime?" Mark was trying to be nice with Nichola. He got down on one knee, like a film comedian. "Why don't you try me out, young lady? You know what most girls say? 'To know me is to love me.'"

"I don't expect," Nichola said dispassionately, "that I shall love anyone, ever again."

"Nichola!" Aunt Tish exclaimed.

Nichola swung round on her, eyes defiant. "I'm not! I loved Papa, and he's gone. I loved Paul, and he's not here any more. And Nannie, and Grandmamma and my pony. A person can't keep taking chances."

"Darling, Papa didn't want to go away. He had to, because of the War. He wanted to take care of you, protect you." Aunt Tish straightened. "We can't protect people by shielding them from things, can we, even when they're small?" She went upstairs, came back pale-faced but composed, carrying a small case. She knelt, putting it in Nichola's hands.

"Open it, Nikki."

The jewels of the medals winked in the summer light.

"His Majesty sent these for you," Aunt Tish said steadily. "That's the Distinguished Flying Cross and the Cross of Valour. They were your father's, because he was very brave. He did his duty, even though it was very hard. He died, Nikki, because he loved us very much and was proud of us and wanted to make the world safe for us all, even if it cost his life. But he wanted you to have these, so you could keep them and know he never stopped loving you."

Nichola closed the case slowly. "And Paul?"

"You'd better tell her," Katie said. Aunt Tish smoothed Nichola's hair.

"Paul is in trouble," she said at last. "He hurt somebody who was cruel to him, though he didn't mean to. You remember how he rescued Captain and chased away that man who was plaguing me?" Nichola nodded. "It was like that, only people didn't understand and thought he was doing something bad. And because of it, he's had to go away awhile. Mark and the girls are trying to help him. They're looking for things he's accused of taking from our houses. Money and Great-Aunt Kate's emerald ring. If they can find them, he'll be in less trouble."

"He didn't want to go away from here, Nichola," I said softly. "He misses you. He sends his love." That was a lie, but he would have done so, if he'd talked to me at all.

Nichola didn't even hear me. She was staring at her mother with that detached, level gaze. Without a word, she turned and walked away.

Aunt Tish started to reach after her; let her arms

fall. "She needs to be alone. She needs to work it through. God knows how long." She pulled herself up, looking tired. "Well, that's that. How do you propose to search?"

Mark outlined the procedure we had used at Gram's, and she nodded. We began working down the length of the living room. Nothing in couch corners; nothing slid under drawers or fallen through cracks.

Katie straightened, rubbing her back. "Nothing here. We'll try the dining room. But kid, I'm afraid it isn't any use."

If the money had been taken, and not lost, it could be anywhere. *But Paul couldn't have.*

Nichola came back, so quietly we did not hear her step on the Persian rug. She came straight to me, holding out a bundle. "Here."

Wrapped in crumpled, monogrammed linen, there they were . . . coins, tightly folded bills, Aunt Kate's little emerald ring.

*"Nichola,"* Aunt Tish said slowly.

"I didn't know the money belonged to anyone. It was just lying around. You said there was plenty of everything here, that I didn't have to worry about food or anything but could have all I want. And the ring's mine. You *told* me it was mine. I thought I could sell it."

"But *why?*" Aunt Tish asked in that disbelieving voice.

Nichola just looked at her. "To get Home," she said. "To get Home and look for Papa. But it's not any use, is it? He isn't there. He isn't anywhere." Her eyes were absolutely dry, and so old, like her mother's. But all at once the little girl in her began to whimper, and her face crumpled, and Aunt Tish whispered, "Oh, darling, he'll always be there with you in your heart," and gathered her in, and we got out of there.

WE DROPPED DOWN UNDER A LARGE TREE IN THE BACK yard, feeling shaken. "Well, that's that," Mark said.

"We still haven't found the lavaliere," Katie said uneasily. "That disappeared before Nikki even got here."

"I keep telling you Paul couldn't have that," I said doggedly. But I could read in Katie's eyes, and Mark's, that my testimony could not exactly be taken as unbiased.

Saturday was Mark's graduation, for which Katie had a new dress and Mother did up her hair. Leslie Skinner was in the city for weekend leave, and on Sunday Gram's house rang with the excitement of Melissa's and Leslie's wedding plans. I tried to show enthusiasm for the pale blue *point d'esprit* bridesmaid's dress that the dressmaker would start to make for me on Monday.

Monday was the first day for Paul to appear in court.

I couldn't get straight exactly what was taking place, although Dad patiently tried to explain. What I did understand was that several things were at stake: whether Paul should be sent to Reform School for trying to kill his father; whether that had actually been his intent; whether he should in any case be made a

Ward of the Court as an incorrigible because his parents were refusing to take further responsibility for him; whether his past history was proof of unwarranted and irredeemable malfeasance.

Early on Monday we went to the white stone court-house, Mother and Dad and I. We met with the district attorney in the lobby outside the courtroom. He seemed pleasant, unvillainous, and he and Dad addressed each other by first names, but once in the courtroom itself formality reigned. Not many people were present. Dad and Mark had succeeded in softpedaling the involvement of Congressman Schuyler's son. Mark was there with his mother, his father being occupied in Washington. Katie and Gram came in, both looking stubborn; Gram had wanted Katie to stay home. The Hodges arrived, he in bandages and truculent, she blowzy and somehow frightened. Dad and Uncle Ben went to the defense table. Aunt Tish slipped into the seat beside me.

The guards brought Paul in.

It was the first I'd seen him since he'd been arrested. He looked terrible; not maltreated, but as though something had died inside. For a moment our eyes locked, then abruptly he broke contact and went to the defense table and sat down. He wore a carefully pressed shirt and pants, and a cardigan sweater that looked suspiciously like Uncle Ben's. Didn't he own a suit? Was that why he came to social events looking as though he didn't care?

The courtroom procedure began. The charge read. Opening remarks of the attorneys . . . the two sides of

Paul Albert Hodge, all of which I had heard before. The parade of defense witnesses beginning. Aunt Tish testified that Paul's evicting the reporter had been in her defense. I corroborated her, told the story as I had seen it of Paul's assault on Mark in the school gym. My attempts to prove extenuating circumstances were overruled.

Dad put Paul on the stand, but Paul did not help himself. He didn't even try. He might have been a million miles away, uncaring, sullen; Aunt Tish and Mother exchanged glances in dismay.

Paul would not tell what his father had said to him that night of the attack. Dad tried every way to force him, but could not. I scribbled a frantic note, *"Tell! I don't care!"* and passed it forward, but he would not read it.

The cross-examination was devastating. So was the parade of prosecution witnesses. Mark gave his testimony as dispassionately as possible, trying to put Paul in the best light, and was repeatedly stopped from making conclusions and value-judgements. He did manage to get onto the record the fact that he had baited Paul, but that was all. The issue, repeatedly defined, was not how Paul Hodge had been treated, but whether his own actions were consistently dangerous.

The reporter's version of his call on Mrs. Maitland-Mayne differed considerably from Aunt Tish's and mine. Mr. Hodge told of the assault on him and had to be constantly hauled back from going off on tangents like the fire.

The fire, for which Paul had not been charged, hung like an invisible guilt above his head.

*Why don't you tell what really happened then?* I wanted to scream at Paul. But I knew why. Because he'd tried to save his father, to do something his father could respect or love him for, and his father hadn't known, hadn't cared, had judged him guilty. Because it was too late now to prove anything. *I* couldn't tell. I had given Paul my solemn vow I would not tell.

"WHY DIDN'T YOU STOP MR. HODGE FROM IMPLYING ALL those awful things?" I exploded to my father when, court adjourned, we went back home. And he replied with maddening calmness, "I did stop him. But Saranne, you know Paul's background is part of the case against him."

"Then if it's history that's on trial, let it be the *whole* history. What's been done to him, not just what he's done. Put somebody on the stand to tell *why* the worst has always been expected of him just because of who he was!"

"Darling, we can't," Mother said patiently.

"Why not? Because there's nothing to tell? I don't believe it!"

I couldn't stay home, not with Aunt Sadie, who'd been with difficulty kept away from court, bound and determined to hear everything that went on. I banged out the screen door and went down to Uncle Ben's house.

Nichola was glad to see me. "She knows," Aunt

Tish said. "I told her all of it. I should have remembered not knowing's always the worst to bear. Stay for dinner, Saranne. It won't be ready for another hour."

Aunt Tish and Uncle Ben were sitting at the table in the quiet kitchen, drinking iced tea somberly.

I looked from one to the other. "We've lost, haven't we?"

"It's too soon to say, honey," Uncle Ben replied.

"You heard it all today. You heard Paul. He's not even fighting."

"Can't blame him much, can you?" my uncle asked quietly. "I guess he's all fought out."

"He's been trying for years to get people's respect . . . and now he's giving up when he'd almost made it."

"Had he?" Uncle Ben asked wryly. "You heard Mr. Hodge. Even his own family's against him. Always has been. That's what's knocked the stuffing out of him, facing the reality of that at last."

"I think the only hope for him could have been Mary." Aunt Tish sighed. "Well, it's too late now. Even if she were willing to take him off her parents' hands, how could she, with her career and all?"

I looked at her, grasping at straws. "Why don't you call her? Mother said you were friends—"

"Not friends. We were involved in each other's lives." Aunt Tish looked at her hands. "I meddled in her life enough when we were young. I can't now, there are things I owe her. The case has been in all the papers. Mary would have come forward if she felt that she could help."

There was the same remote expression on my uncle's face.

I wandered out to the porch, sat down in the hanging swing, and closed my eyes. There was nothing more to do. Paul needed a last-minute Portia to the rescue— well, we'd tried. And we had failed. Nothing remained now but the wrapping-up.

There was a pile of magazines on the wicker table. I picked some up. Anything to dull my mind and drive out the shadows that were haunting it.

They were the old *Literary Quarterlies* from Gram's attic. Aunt Tish must have brought them over; they were from her high school writing years. I started reading, at first dispiritedly and then with growing interest as I began to recognize West Farms places and characters. Eventually, I came upon a story with the by-line of Mary Hodge. No one had ever told me she once wrote.

I began to read, and as I did a hammering began inside my head. Mary had written the story of an unwanted child. A baby, being born unexpectedly, hoping to be loved, but coming into a world that had no place for it. A baby that society said ought not to have been born.

She might have been writing about Paul. But how could she have known what life would be like for him as he grew? The story had been written—I looked at the cover; Spring 1902—a few months after Paul was born.

Mary Hodge, writing in 1902 with such anguish, about an unwanted child. Paul Hodge, born an unwanted baby in the fall of 1901.

Mr. Hodge, throwing it up to Paul about bad blood, about how he should be grateful to them. Asking, obscenely, about Paul and me; mumbling about history repeating.

Aunt Sadie, asking what anybody could expect. The whole neighborhood so sure that Paul was bound to turn out bad . . . everyone who had known the Hodges when he was born. My recurring, nagging feeling of a hidden secret.

I put the magazine down slowly, my heart pounding, unable even to formulate in words the direction in which my mind was leaping. Then *I* was leaping up, running inside, startling my aunt and uncle.

"This is it, isn't it?" I thrust the magazine beneath their noses. "This is why the—the persecution, Mr. Hodge's hatred, everybody keeping their mouths shut so tight."

"I didn't know that magazine was in the stack," Aunt Tish said in a tight voice.

"Suppose you spell out what you think you've added up," Uncle Ben said calmly.

I told him. Flatly. "So there is somebody who could still help Paul, isn't there? Why don't you subpoena her, get her on the phone, anything! You're one of Paul's lawyers, why aren't you helping him?"

"Because we don't have the right to," Aunt Tish said. "Not the way you mean. Even if what you think were true, it could only make things worse."

"It couldn't. There *is* no worse." I stared at them,

hopelessly, and then I swung around, grappling frantically with my purse.

"Darling, what are you doing?" Aunt Tish demanded.

"I'm going to find Mary Hayes. She's in Fort Lee
somewhere. Maybe I don't have the right to, either, but
I care what happens to Paul."

Uncle Ben rose. "That could be the one thing that
makes the difference. Come on, Saranne, if you're determined to go through with this, I'll take you."

We motored in near-silence downtown, past Central Park to the ferry dock, across to Weehawken, up the
steep drive to the top of the Palisades. Then north along
the river, through small towns clustered high above the
water's edge.

"How far *is* it?" I asked, and Uncle Ben turned
briefly to smile at me.

"Not far."

"How can we ever find her—"

"We will, if we have to knock at the door of every
boarding house in Fort Lee."

We were in luck. The film studio was shooting late,
taking advantage of the long June light. Uncle Ben
pulled up before the studio's wooden barricade and
leaned out.

"Can you tell me where I might find Miss Mary
Hayes?"

The gatekeeper shifted the chewing gum in his
mouth and shrugged. "They're shooting on the bluff,
but visitors aren't allowed."

"Oh, I think she'll see me," Uncle Ben said easily, holding out his attorney's business card. After that, the man made no trouble.

We rolled down a street lined with false facades. A few passers-by, heavily made up, eyed us curiously but did not stop us. Beyond the scenery, in an open field, there was a flurry of activity. A man raced up to us as we approached. "You can't go out there! They're filming."

Uncle Ben repeated his business with explanation and card. The man nodded, left. We waited. After several moments a slight figure detached itself from the knot of people and came running toward us. She looked half a child, in girlish dress and tousled red-gold curls; it was not till she was very close that I could see faint lines around her eyes.

"Ben! Oh, good heavens, Ben, it's been so long!"

"How are you, Mary?" Uncle Ben said, and hugged her.

"It's so good to see somebody from home. What brought—" Her face altered. "Nothing's happened to Mama?"

"No. Saranne, Bron's girl, wants to talk to you. Mary, you know about the trial?"

"Yes." She stiffened slightly, became guarded, wary. "Poor Paul. I hope to God it's going to work out all right."

"We're trying. At least, Sidney and I are, as much as Paul will let us. He's doing the family 'what the hell's the use' act. Remember?" Mary nodded faintly, and Ben went on deliberately, watching her. "It doesn't look good, Mary. Everything he's ever done and not done's been dragged in as evidence against his character."

Mary's voice had the same bitter edge as Paul's. "Good old West Farms. Some things never change."

"*You* did. And Paul had, really. You can be proud of him, Mary, he's almost made it. Only now your father, blast his hide, is determined to get rid of him forever. If it weren't for the damning fact that your own father keeps ranting on about how he's afraid of him, he could get off lightly."

"The old bastard." Mary's face was yellow-pale. "Did you ever hear, Ben, about *our* last row?"

"I remember," Uncle Ben said astonishingly, "you had a date with me the next night, and you never showed up. You never even wrote."

"I couldn't. It just seemed the best thing I could do was to get out of everybody's lives before I pulled the rest of you down with me." Her voice was the echo of Paul's words to me. "Ben, if I hadn't run, right that night, *I* might have killed him. He called me—oh, well, it's all water under the bridge now, isn't it? But he'll never forgive me, ever, for anything. He's mean. If my father's determined, Paul hasn't got a chance against him."

"*But you would.*" The words burst from me. My pulses were pounding, but I poured it out frantically before I could lose my nerve. "It's the fact that his own father won't take responsibility for him that's making all the trouble. Your mother, too, but she's just dazed, just going along. It's your father who's disowning him, and Paul's so alone, he's got nobody to turn to but me, and I don't count. He won't even *let* me help, because he thinks he's hurt me. But *you* could stand up for him, you're his blood kin, you know what he's gone through and why. If you were willing to be his guardian—"

I half expected Mary to cut me off. But when she interrupted, she was almost pleading. "I can't. Lord knows I've thought of it. I've always wished—but I'm on my own, a gypsy life, and I've only myself to rely on. I have to think of my career. Paul's better off in West Farms."

"Not if he hasn't a home. Or is in jail."

"*I can't.* And even if I offered—" Mary shrugged. It was meant to be reckless and gallant, but I sensed the fear, just as I had so often sensed the same pain and fear in Paul. "I'm not exactly a pillar of society. I ran away at an early age and went on the wicked screen. No judge in his senses would think I had the right to ask to be guardian of a troubled kid."

Uncle Ben had not said a word. He was leaving it up to me, just as he'd said he had to. And with a sick feeling in my stomach I could understand why he and Aunt Tish had felt they could not butt in, must respect the conspiracy of silence because Mary was their friend. But Paul was my friend.

"You do have the right, don't you? The best right of all." I stopped, my throat dry, and I knew that forever after I was going to remember that look on Mary's face.

"You're his mother, aren't you?" I said at last. "You're his real mother. That's the secret West Farms has been keeping from him for sixteen years."

# June

# X

MARY DIDN'T SPEAK. SHE JUST TURNED AWAY SLIGHTLY
and put her hand to her head as if she were very tired.

"Even if—what you think you know—were true,"
she said at last, "I don't see why you think it would help
my coming forward. The court would never appoint
me guardian. Not now."

"I'm not so sure about that," Uncle Ben said casually.

She went on as if he hadn't spoken. "And Paul has
had enough disgrace."

"He's had enough rejection from supposed loving
parents," Uncle Ben said in that same voice.

And I added swiftly, "I don't think anything, *anything* could make things worse for him than they are
just now. Or anything help him, except having somebody who does have a blood bond with him stand by
him."

"Anyway, the whole idea's ridiculous. I'm not what

you think, I don't know where you got the idea—" She swung round suddenly, her eyes filled with horror. "Ben, not you—"

I held out the magazine, and Mary looked at it and laughed. She laughed until the laughter turned to choking sobs, and she dropped down on the ground, her arms hugged tight. I stood in an agony of embarrassment, not knowing where to look, and Uncle Ben knelt and put his arms around her.

"I think it's time the charade was dropped. No, no one told. Saranne just put two and two together, and she and Katie and Mark Schuyler have been doing a nice piece of detective work looking for evidence to exonerate Paul. You can be glad your son has such good friends."

Mary nodded and wiped her eyes. "But I still can't do anything. Even if I dared risk it, the court wouldn't give him to me now."

"You could *be* there," Ben said. "You could show that his family has not all turned against him. That would mean something, Mary, and not just to Paul. You'd be surprised how many there are who admire the way you've turned your life around and made something of it."

Mary looked at him steadily. "If I do what you ask, everything could go down the drain."

"Would it?" Ben asked quizzically. "And Mary, you're forgetting something. *I'm* not the one asking. Saranne is. Because she loves Paul. The girl I knew could understand about demanding painful things to help those you love."

"The girl you knew's been gone a long time, Ben."
Mary made a brief flicking gesture with her fingers. "My
career could go now, just like that. Movies are family
entertainment. The public wants its illusions, not stars
with sordid pasts, illegitimate children." It was toward
Uncle Ben she was arguing, not me, but Uncle Ben did
not say a word, he just kept looking at her, and after a
stillness she drew a deep breath.

"All right. I'll go with you. Just to be at the trial
as moral support for Paul, that's all I can promise."

We drove Mary, after a brief *sotto voce* argument
with her director, to her boarding house and waited on
the porch while she packed some clothes. We rode back
to New York, scarcely speaking. We hadn't had dinner;
we none of us thought of food. We went straight to
Uncle Ben's house, where Aunt Tish stood silhouetted
in the open doorway to welcome Mary in.

They looked at each other for a long moment, and
Tish said, "It's been a long time. I'm glad you've come,"
and Mary nodded.

"I heard about your husband. Tish, I'm sorry."

Uncle Ben went to the telephone to call my father.
"Sidney? Our miracle came through; Mary's here. You'd
better come."

I didn't belong there. I ran home, and Mother
heated supper for me and kept Aunt Sadie away. I went
to bed and prayed a lot.

WHEN WE GOT TO COURT NEXT MORNING, KATIE CAME
dashing up. "What happened? I kept calling your house
last night, and Bron said you were out, and then asleep."

"I had a headache. Katie, please, I just can't talk." Katie looked at me and, like Mother before her, was silent.

The courtroom was much the same as yesterday. The same faces. The same sunlight. Paul in the same outfit, heartbreakingly neat, his eyes distant, not even seeing me.

Uncle Ben was not yet there. Just after the clerk called the court to order, the leather door opened and he came in, and Aunt Tish and Mary Hayes were with him.

There were no tousled curls today, the red-gold hair was up in a twist beneath a summer hat. Mary Hayes, like Aunt Tish, wore delicate white, but she had the same heartbreaking look of effort to her as did Paul. She and Tish took seats by me and Mother, as a belated recognition stirred the hall.

Mrs. Hodge, in blue and white stripe with ruffles, froze in the act of fanning herself, like a figure in a silly childhood game. Mr. Hodge, peering to see what the distraction was, saw Mary just as Mary turned toward him.

I had thought I knew what hatred was after these past months, after hearing Paul do the speech about "I am a Jew." I had never felt it so naked and crackling as I did now.

Only a moment, and then Mary, her eyes closed, turned away, her actor's training making her seem perfectly serene.

Paul saw none of this. Paul didn't look.

The case resumed. The parade of witnesses continued. I waited, scarcely breathing. It looked bad. It looked very bad. Before us, I could feel Dad and Uncle Ben waiting, too, for an interruption that did not come.

The judge looked at Dad over his glasses. "If there are no further witnesses for the defense, we will hear closing arguments."

The district attorney summed up his case. Listening, I had that strange disassociated feeling that I had had sometimes at play rehearsals. If I did not know Paul, truly know him, what would I believe? The portrait of him was at once so accurate and so wrong.

One swift movement beside me. Mary Hayes, pulling at my uncle's arm. "Put me on the stand. I'll ask for custody."

My lungs hurt with relief as I let out my breath. Mother slid a swift, understanding arm around me.

Uncle Ben rose. "Your honor, before making a closing statement, I must tell you that someone has come forward to petition for guardianship of Paul Hodge. She will assume this responsibility, if the court remands him to her custody."

"Who is that?"

"His sister, Mary Hayes."

A ripple through the court. Mrs. Hodge's mouth, slack with astonishment, and something more. The district attorney, caught off-guard.

Mary Hayes on the witness stand, giving her name, her address, her occupation, Paul, after one startled glance, dropping his eyes again. Ben, leading Mary through a recital of why she felt she could provide suitable guardianship.

"We were raised in the same home, so I feel I am in as . . . a better position than most to understand the circumstances that have brought Paul to this present situation." Mary's gaze turned briefly toward her parents. The sunlight, touching her copper hair, made her look like a Mary Pickford Sweetheart, but her eyes were so accusing and so old.

Mrs. Hodge's hands kept clenching and unclenching. Mr. Hodge looked as though he needed a drink.

The testimony, couched in courtroom terms, sounded as formal as a play. "I am under long-term contract and in a position to support a ward. As far as my profession, contrary to what the public thinks, a very family atmosphere prevails. There are many minors involved, either directly or as children of my colleagues, who have had a healthy upbringing in the environment."

The judge leaned forward.

"The court is appreciative of the offer, and the sisterly affection in which it is made. But I cannot feel this would be a suitable solution. The defendant has been demonstrated to be incorrigible, and a physical danger to himself and others. We cannot in conscience turn him loose in society at the present time, not when his parents, who have primary responsibility for him, cannot control him."

Paul sat doodling, paying no attention, not even caring.

A look passed back and forth between Uncle Ben and Mary.

"Miss Hayes," Uncle Ben said quietly, "you've just heard the court's considered judgement. Will you tell the court why you think Paul Hodge should be placed in your guardianship, despite the fact that Grace and Albert Hodge are not willing to act as parents to him any longer?"

Mary Hayes was looking straight at Paul. "Because I have the primary responsibility. I'm his mother."

Paul didn't move, not a muscle. He just stared at her, with nothing showing at all. Mother leaned forward. "She did it, she really did it," she whispered to Aunt Tish, who just nodded, her gaze never leaving Mary.

The judge was gaveling. Everything reverted incongruously to routine. Uncle Ben was taking Mary matter-of-factly through the story. "Fifteen years old . . . discovered I was having a child by someone who was not in a position to marry me." (Who, I wondered, as I had been wondering the past twenty-four hours. I knew I could never ask.) "Parents were frantic . . . horrified at the disgrace . . . determined I should have the child elsewhere, claiming I was away at school, and that the baby's birth certificate should show the baby as being theirs."

The bare bones of story, stripped of emotion, tore my heart.

"Did you want to give up your child?"

"No. I had no choice. I had to promise my parents

. . . that if they cared for him . . . I would never make any claim on him again."

"And in your judgement, Miss Hayes, is it these facts surrounding your son's birth that caused your parents, and much of this community that knew the story but joined through kindness in a conspiracy of silence, to *expect* your son to 'go bad'? To have 'bad blood,' to be 'rotten from birth' as your father alleged? Do you believe that rather than being vicious and incapable of control, your son was pressured by forces he could not understand—that he was judged before he proved himself, his every action interpreted in the light of expected 'badness'? And that these attacks of physical violence of which we have heard were the inevitable result, not of his own nature, but of the treatment he received?"

"Yes. Oh, yes."

Dad turned to the bench. "Your honor, Miss Hayes is aware of the names and addresses of the persons who attended her in her confinement. If necessary, they can be subpoenaed to identify her as the actual 'Mrs. Albert Hodge' who gave birth to the defendant Paul Albert Hodge in October, 1901."

It would not be necessary, unless for some dry requirement of the records. Mrs. Hodge had lumbered to her feet, tears running down her pathetically unlovely face. "You promised. You promised you'd never tell he was yours, and now you've done it. Haven't we been disgraced enough already?"

More gaveling. Mary turned her head away and closed her eyes. I wanted to throw my arms around Paul and melt the ice of him, but I could not. Would he hate me, for having brought this out?

In a strange way, that was not important.

What was important was the judge, looking at Paul, at Mary, above his glasses. Saying the action on the assault charge would be postponed pending the filing of the guardianship petition. "And young man, whether you want me to or not, I'm going to release you on the bail offered by your attorney, into the custody of your mother."

Court was dismissed.

Mary was still sitting on the witness stand. She rose tentatively, looking at Paul, as if she didn't know what to expect. He, too, rose slowly. Dad touched my arm and said gently, "Come on now, honey," and I turned and went.

Out in the hall I could hear vaguely the murmurs of spectators, the startled questions pouring out of Katie. No reporters were there, fortunately. But if they found out, what would this do to Mary Hayes's career? She'd burned her bridges. What was worse for Paul, the familiar burden of rejection by the Hodges, of feeling he had, as he'd said, "a devil in him"? Or the discovery of illegitimacy, of having been lied to all these years? Of being the scapegoat for his real mother's fall from grace? Would he forgvie me for ripping the lid off this can of worms at last?

Mr. Hodge pushed past us, cursing beneath his breath. Mrs. Hodge came out, miserably. Gram went to her, and they touched briefly without speaking. Aunt

Tish came to me, her face mirroring all that I was feeling. We just looked at each other, and then she hugged me hard.

"Don't you think we should go?" Mother said. I shook my head. Behind me there was a whisper of moving air: the courtroom doors opening and closing. I turned.

Paul stood there. Mary was behind him, sensitive as I had been about not pushing in. I looked at him, and he looked at me, and I knew that they didn't matter— all the things done and undone, understood and not —that what we had between us had not been destroyed. If anything, it had grown stronger.

He only touched my hands a moment. Then he and Mary were gone.

I felt lightheaded, as though I were recovering from the flu. It was Gram, the ever-practical, who broke the spell. "Don't know about the rest of you, but I'm half-starved. Let's stop at a cafe somewhere and have second breakfast."

We did. Then at home the telephone started ringing. The West Farm grapevine, springing into action. . . . Melissa was dashing around, engrossed in wedding plans. The dressmaker grabbed Katie and me for fittings. Life went on.

Life went on, in its haphazard, unpredictable Sterling pattern. Paul and Mary did not go back to Uncle Ben's. No one knew where they went, they just vanished. By a miracle I knew better than to ask about, the Mary Hayes–Paul Hodge revelation had been kept out of the press. And in a few days, West Farms attention turned to Melissa's wedding, now a week and a half away.

The Saturday of Melissa and Leslie's wedding came almost too soon. The Skinners were staying at our house, Aunt Annie and Uncle Will, and Leslie's sister Alice, who was to be Melissa's maid of honor. I laughed with the others and bubbled with excitement along with Katie when she and I and two of Melissa's school chums hooked each other into our pale blue bridesmaid's dresses.

It was an afternoon wedding at Grace Church, performed by Mr. Derbyshire, who had married Mother and Aunt Marnie, who had baptized and confirmed us all. And at Melissa's special request, Mother sang.

There was a flurry in the vestibule as we formed for the procession. Melissa was radiant, wearing Mother's lace veil. Watch one's step, move straight ahead, don't look down. . . .

The vows . . . the pronouncement of marriage, the benediction, the recessional. Bells ringing. Tears and laughter. Back to Gram's, where the furniture was stashed in cellar and attic, and the lace and embroidered cloths were spread, and crystal glistened in the afternoon sun. All the loved, familiar family traditions. (How was Aunt Tish feeling, at this first wedding after Anthony was gone? Her own had been so many miles away.)

The wedding buffet was spread in the double parlors, but punch and cookies were served also on the lawn. There was dancing on the porch—Katie, circling dreamily with Mark; me, waltzing with Tim.

"I know I'm not the preferred partner, but I'll fill in," he said. "How is Paul, Saranne?"

"I don't know."

"Don't worry," he said comfortably. "He'll be OK."

Was it terribly selfish to want Paul not only all right, but *there*.

The dance ended; another began. Mark cut in. "Katie told me about your part in the grand Hodge denouement. You're quite a girl, Sarah Anne Albright. That was a pretty great thing you did."

"It was a pretty great thing you did yourself, getting us mobilized to clear Paul of those theft charges."

"That necklace of Katie's still hasn't shown up, has it?" I just stared at him and Mark added hastily, "I didn't mean anything! I *know* Paul's innocent. It would just be good to have all the loose ends tied up."

Neatly. Tidily. Nicely. The way Paul's life was, in everybody's eyes. Paul was out of the Hodge house, probably forever. It was probably the best thing for him, and it was definitely selfish of me to wish that he were back. What was it Uncle Ben had said that day on the bluffs to Mary—how really loving people meant being willing to endure the pain of what was best for them?

I stopped dancing, and Mark sensed my mood and steered me down the steps. On the lawn, all the younger Sterling kids were playing, but I was safe from too-knowing older eyes. Nichola, in her Easter dress, was engaged in earnest make-believe with the quietest of Aunt Marnie's brood, interrupted by Iago's raucous nosiness. The others, taking advantage of parental absence, were playing follow-the-leader to the detriment of their Sunday clothes. Jimmie Jr. led the way up the old apple tree beside the porch.

"Hey, be careful there," Mark called, and then, "Oh-oh!" A low branch with three cousins aboard it cracked, spilling them to the ground. We rushed over.

"No bones broken," Mark said, examining the boys while I wiped off their tears. "You OK, old man?"

Jimmy Jr. nodded, hiccuping. "Gram's gonna be mad. And Iago. That's his favorite perch."

We looked upward, to where the branch had separated from Iago's knothole. And I caught my breath.

"Jimmy," I said carefully, "you want to get back in Gram's good graces? Do you see that glitter in the hole? Can you shinny up and get whatever it is?"

He did. Came back, face beaming, and held out his hands. A rusty bell from an old child's toy. Some coins. A bright green glass button. An amethyst, winking in a filigree gold frame.

"What fools we were," Mark said ironically. "*Iago.* Of course. Crows love bright things, and he was all over the place in the house that night.

I picked up Katie's lavaliere with shaking fingers. Such a little thing, to have precipitated so much.

If only there was a way to let Paul know. *Paul. . . .*

The music was floating around us, "Long, Long Trail." *There's a long long night of waiting until my dreams all come true . . .*

I dropped the lavaliere into Mark's hands. "Give it to Katie, will you?" I murmured, and fled down past the lilac bushes and across the lawn. Aunt Tish was strolling quietly with Mr. Latham; she looked up at me with a grave smile that understood exactly what I was feeling.

It was quieter in the small patch of lawn beyond the roses that connected Gram's yard with that of Uncle Ben's house. I stopped, leaning against the coolness of a tree . . . the tree Paul had stood smoking under, the night of the party so many months ago. I closed my eyes, and I could see him there—the arrogant pose that I knew now was armor of bravado, the blue eyes that could blaze with such a gamut of emotions, the leprechaun hair.

I opened my eyes, and Paul was coming toward me through the roses.

"I thought you'd be here," he said simply. "I had to see you." For a moment we just looked at each other with that space between us, and then there was no need for speech, and no space at all.

"STRANGE," PAUL SAID PRESENTLY, WHEN I ASKED HIM how he felt. "Like I've come out of a dark forest and have to get my eyes used to the light." He looked at me. "Mary told me what you did, going to Fort Lee."

"I was so afraid you'd hate me for it."

"I think I've lost the ability to hate," Paul said in a kind of wonder. "It's like a weight's off, now I'm free of that house forever . . . I don't even have an impulse for revenge. I could never imagine what it was like, not to want revenge."

"I can't imagine what it was like for you to want it."

"No. Meanness is not part of your nature, is it? That's one of the things that hooked me, you're so nice." He said it teasingly, then grew serious when he saw me wince. "I mean it. Decent, honorable, kind. Maybe they don't sound like much as compliments, but they mean a lot to me."

"Now you're embarrassing me."

"Maybe it sounds better as poetry," Paul said wickedly, and he quoted a line from our late play. " 'How far that little candle throws its beams! So shines a good deed in a naughty world.' "

"Maybe," I said, "we ought to go in to the wedding party."

"Mary's there. She's got guts, hasn't she?" Paul said. "Saranne—I think it's going to work out."

"No more 'wild Hodge boy'?" I said it lightly, but I meant a whole lot more, and Paul knew it. He shook his head.

"I'm not afraid of the 'devil in me' any more. There's a long way to go, but I've come a long way already. Thanks to you." Paul gave me a slanting glance. "Of course, I don't know as I want to stop being wild, completely." He took me in his arms.

I knew then that labels have nothing to do with people. The Paul Hodge in his new linen suit who walked with me into the garden where Katie and Mark and Nichola were waiting was so much more than just "that wild Hodge boy." And "nice little girl" was not an adequate term for me at all.